"These stories bristle  the
bone. With imagery   uar-
iums, Ross evokes th   r of

T0154833   _ack!_

"Whipsmart and lightning quick in their prose, these stories dance along the same razor's edge as us all, balanced
between everyday life and the outlandish, absurd, and
sobering certainty of its end. Michelle Ross is an important
new talent, a companionable, wise, and often-funny voice
for these troubled times. I will be eagerly assigning this
book to students and pressing it into the hands of my most
devoted reader friends."

—Robin Black, author of
If I Loved You, I Would Tell You This

"Michelle Ross' exceptional first collection traffics in dark
matter, the murky material that we sense but cannot see,
the unconscious and peripheral parts of life that affect us
as surely as the parts we recognize as real and concrete. In
the uncomfortable spaces of a woman trapped (literally
and metaphorically) in a soul-crushing job, another hiding
from a shooter (real? imagined?) in a closet full of six-year-
olds, a girl playing serial killer/victim, or a family fighting
over the cremated remains of a loved one at the rattlesnake
roundup, Ross digs down to find truth—never afraid of
the dirt and grime that, ultimately, give way to moments
of grace. Her scientific eye for detail, humor, and humanity
blend in stories that are grotesque, compelling, and deeply
affecting. An astonishing and accomplished debut."

—Alison Umminger, author of
American Girls

THERE'S SO MUCH THEY HAVEN'T TOLD YOU

MICHELLE ROSS

MOON CITY PRESS
Department of English
Missouri State University
901 South National Avenue
Springfield, Missouri 65897

Published by Moon City Press, Springfield, Missouri, USA, in 2016.

Library of Congress Cataloging-in-Publication Data

Ross, Michelle N.
There's So Much They Haven't Told You: Stories/Michelle Ross, 1976–

2016917973

Further Library of Congress information is available upon request.

ISBN-10: 0-913785-88-1
ISBN-13: 978-0-913785-88-1

Cover and interior designed by Charli Barnes

Edited by Joel Coltharp & Michael Czyzniejewski
Text copyedited by Karen Craigo

Manufactured in the United States of America.

www.mooncitypress.com

Versions of these stories have previously appeared elsewhere: "Atoms" in *Hobart*; "If My Mother Was the Final Girl" in *Gulf Coast*; "Prologue" in *Gravel*; "Alien Eye" in *The Nervous Breakdown*; "Like Pulling Teeth" in *Necessary Fiction*; "How Many Ways Can You Die on a Bus?" in the *Main Street Rag* anthology, *Slower Traffic Keep Right*; "Sex Ed." in *Bird's Thumb*; "If You Were a Serial Killer" in *The Adroit Journal*; "Unit 7: Exploring Fossils" in *Synaesthesia Magazine*; "Rattlesnake Roundup" in *Moon City Review*; "Pam's Head" in *The Journal of Compressed Creative Arts*; "Key Concepts in Ecology" in *The Common*; "Ventriloquy" in *Pebble Lake Review*; "When the Cottonmouths Come to Feed" in *Cream City Review*; "An Impromptu Lesson on Black Holes" in *The Indianola Review*; "The Nature of Light" in *Blue Lake Review*; "Kinetic Theory" in *Fiction Southeast*; "Taxidermy Q&A" (previously "Dear Chester") in *Faultline*; "Stories People Tell" in *Superstition Review*; "Virgins" in *Arroyo Literary Review*; "Of All the Animals in the Aquarium" in *SmokeLong Quarterly*; "Cinéma Vérité" in *Sixfold*; and "Transactions" in *Fiction Southeast*.

ACKNOWLEDGEMENTS

Thank you so much to everyone at Moon City Press for their hard work and expertise in making this book a beautiful thing, especially Michael Czyzniejewski, Joel Coltharp, Karen Craigo, and Charli Barnes. Their enthusiasm means the world to me.

Thank you to Robin Black, Kathleen Founds, Gina Frangello, Aubrey Hirsch, Dana Johnson, David James Poissant, Eric Puchner, and Amber Sparks for their generous praise.

Thank you to my teachers: Aldo Alvarez, Marshall Klimasewiski, Carol Lee Lorenzo, Alyce Miller, Cornelia Nixon, and especially to Tony Ardizzone and Lynna Williams.

Thank you to all the editors and contest judges who have given these stories homes over the years and who, in doing so, gave me faith. Special thanks to those editors who have helped shape and strengthen these stories and to those editors whose strong support of my work has been particularly energizing: Jennifer Acker, Georgia Bellas, Annabelle Carvell, Lenae Souza Crowder, Anita Dellaria, Carlotta Eden, Elizabeth Ellen, Sherri H. Hoffman, Katie Flynn, Christie Frakes, and Sahar Mustafah.

Thank you to Dan Cafaro for giving *me* a home at *Atticus Review*.

Thank you to the books and films that have inspired some of these stories, especially Carol Clover's *Men, Women, and Chain Saws: Gender in the Modern Horror Film*.

Thank you to Eleanor Gallagher, Thaila Ramanujam, Alice Ritscherle, and Alison Umminger for their invaluable critiques and support for this book. Thank you to Margaret Ronda: the first several stories that I published owe much to her. Thank you to Kim Magowan, whose hand is all over this book and who has been a huge inspiration and champion of my writing. Thank you to Brandi Rogers, my earliest advocate, who has been reading my stories for nearly twenty years. Thank you to all for your friendship.

And thank you to Chris and Atticus, who put up with me day after day: It's not easy living with a writer, maybe especially this one.

CONTENTS

THERE'S SO MUCH THEY HAVEN'T TOLD YOU

MICHELLE ROSS

ATOMS

You go to school and you go to school and what you're given are tiny bites that don't feel like much of anything in your mouth. But then one day, your science teacher says that everything in the world is made up of the same basic components, called atoms. The universe is like an elaborate Lego structure, she says. "When you get right down to it, it's all just studs and holes." Your classmates snicker.

It's as though your teacher has taken the pot she's been feeding you spoonfuls from and poured it over your head.

"Why did you keep this from us for so long?" you ask her.

"We hadn't gotten to the unit on matter," she says.

You say to your parents, "How come you never told me about atoms?"

Your mother, who is plucking pill bugs from the garden and dropping them into a saucer of beer, says, "I figured your teachers know better than I do when you're ready for that sort of information."

Your father pounds plastic-wrapped chicken breast with his fist. He says, "I never told you about atoms? Hmm."

A boy in your science class starts sitting behind you on the school bus. He whispers into your hair that he's known about atoms for as long as he can remember.

"Man, what else don't you know?" He looks at you like you're the last bite of something delicious.

What else you don't know is this: Nothing is *solid* in the way you formerly understood solid. It is mostly empty space, your teacher says. Everything is mostly empty space. *You* are mostly empty space. "Ponder this," she says, and she's looking directly at you.

"She's right," the boy says that afternoon on the bus ride home, and he blows a long, slow stream of air against the back of your head, and you wish it would never end.

Another day, your teacher says that the parts of your body that are not empty space are not all you, that there are other organisms, too. In fact, bacterial cells outnumber muscle cells and skin cells and bone cells. You are a walking ecosystem.

"Knew that, too," the boy on the bus says. He takes a hunk of your hair and puts it in his mouth.

"Hey," you say.

"What makes you think this hair is even yours? It's more bacteria and fungi than anything else probably, and I don't think they mind the least little bit being in my mouth." His voice comes out muffled with all that hair in the way.

Your teacher calls you by name, but you don't hear her, and she has to say your name again and again before you look up and say, "What?"

She tells you to come up to the board and fill in the part of the Venn diagram where viruses overlap with living things.

You stand there and you stand there, the chalk shedding molecules all over your skin, molecules composed of calcium, carbon, and oxygen atoms, all atoms you already possess. You can no longer see the lines between things.

The boy, he's grinning at you from the back of the

classroom when you look up.

Later, on the bus, he says, "You left the Venn's vaginal slit empty."

You blush. "Nothing makes sense anymore."

"Classification is bullshit," he says.

The boy doesn't stand up when the bus reaches his stop.

Then a few minutes later, he follows you off the bus. The kids who normally exit the bus with you take off toward their houses, but you stand there and look at the boy. If he were to push you, you wouldn't even have to lift a finger or lean your body into it for him to experience an equal and opposite push from you: Newton's third law.

"What are you doing?" you say.

He pulls two lollipops from his backpack. He offers you one.

With the lollipop filling his left cheek like a hidden eyeball, he says, "There's so much more they haven't told you. Don't you want to know?"

IF MY MOTHER
WAS THE FINAL GIRL

> *"... in the end, bloody and staggering,*
> *she finds the highway."*
> —*Carol Clover*

Our Story

My mother's laugh echoes. It's Disney sinister, like a witch peeping her head into the magic cauldron to see that the hawks' beaks and chickens' hearts are brewing as they should.

Her face is buried inside a humidifier-like contraption, which sits on the coffee table like an altar. What I see is a large plastic box topped with curly, frosted hair.

I'm watching a program in which a psychic helps people communicate with their dead relatives. I don't laugh along with my mother, though I too am skeptical.

It's New Year's Eve, and I'm waiting for the microwave to beep. We were supposed to go out for dinner, but my mother has one of her headaches. It's her sinuses that are the problem. They're always blocked.

These headaches make her lose her appetite. They're so bad sometimes that she doesn't move for hours. She lies on the couch, and closed, her eyes look more pained than when open. It's like she's trying to push the headache out through her forehead, like pushing out a baby.

The contraption her face has disappeared into is new to my mother's collection of headache helpers. There's the rice bag that she heats in the microwave and wraps around her neck. There's the eye patch filled with a green liquid. There's the headband with magnets stitched into it. And there's the dish that she heats and fills with therapeutic oils that are supposed to open her breathing passages and relax her muscles.

These things help a little, but never enough. She's looking for the invention that takes her headaches away forever. She'll collect every gadget she can get her hands on until she finds it, even if it means she can open up her own museum.

She discovered most of these products on television. Half the contents of our apartment, from kitchen gadgets to electric wall art, are wonders she saw demonstrated on television. I hate that. I think it's tacky, and I've told her so.

I'm lucky I don't have an apartment of my own, according to my mother. She knows a woman who put her fifteen-year-old daughter up in her own apartment because they couldn't stand the sight of each other. There are days when my mother swears that if she had the money she'd do the same thing. In another year I'll be eighteen, old enough for her to kick me out legally. She's made note of this fact on a number of occasions.

The one thing my mother and I share is a love for slasher films. When the first girl gets hacked up or sawed in half or stabbed in the breast, my mother says, "Now there's real life for you." And I glance at her sideways and think, You can say that again.

The Final Girl

What you have to understand if you're going to appreciate slasher films is that one, there is slasher etiquette; and two, the killer and the final girl are inextricably linked. The chief rule in slasher etiquette is that you laugh at neither of them.

What can you laugh at? The teenagers who decide it's a good idea to have sex in the woods. Bimbo victims who slip and fall as they're running away in high heels. Or very sad, pathetic attempts at killing, like shrunken old grandpa in *The Texas Chain Saw Massacre*, but there is always pain behind *that* laughter.

And the final girl? The killer? They're nearly one and the same. They're the two characters you can't help but identify with. When the final girl is hiding in a closet that the killer is trying to break open, you're in there with her as his knife slashes through each wooden slat. Her too-loud breathing is yours.

But you're also out there with him as he approaches that door. You understand his rage, his desperation. You remember when he too was intruded upon, attacked—when someone broke into his house and screamed at him. He is as scared as she is. Fear and violence reproduce themselves. Or at the very least there's the trauma that lasts forever and ever. And so you know that at the end when the final girl escapes, she hasn't really. She's bound to the killer in a way that the truck she jumps in back of can't save her from. She will take the killer with her wherever she goes. She will never not be afraid. She will never not be angry. And this neverendingness will wear her out. It will ruin her. And she knows it. But there's nothing she can do about it.

Our Story

New Year's morning my mother says she has to get out of this apartment before it kills her. She gives me an accusatory look, as if I have held her here against her will. It's not worth mentioning that we didn't leave the apartment the day before because of *her* headache. I ended up taking NyQuil and going to bed at eleven. I'm as stifled by this space as she is.

"You coming?" she asks.

It's bleak out there, too. The sky is a sickly yellow. It's the color that's left when a bug dies on a windshield. It's the color of a sharp blow to the head.

The snow is two weeks old, and it is anything but clean. It's the kind of weather people disappear in. I want to turn myself inside out, wring, and start over.

"Why not?" I tell her.

At the casino, she takes out forty dollars for herself before handing her wallet to me.

"If I ask for more money, don't let me have it. Forty's my limit. If I can't win with forty, then it's just not meant to be."

I'm not old enough to gamble, not that I would anyway, so that means I sit in the buffet and read. Mostly the food is bland, but it's hard to go wrong with ice cream and all the toppings you want. I have bowl after bowl until I feel ill. My waiter, who wears the requisite New Year's star-spangled hat, gives me a packet of antacids with the check. He tells me his name is Julian, and he wants to know if I'll be there this evening for the New Year's Day party. They're going to have a band and champagne and dancing.

"All the works," he says.

When my mother is empty-handed, she collapses onto the chair across from me, as if she has been trying to twist the lid off a jar that has exhausted and defeated her.

"You know the next nickel that goes into that machine is going to win," she says.

"Mmm," I say.

She doesn't ask me for her wallet, but she muses aloud as to whether she should play just twenty more dollars' worth. I am silent, which only irritates her further. She told me once that when I don't say anything I seem like even more of a snob than when I do.

The Killer

All I know are these details: her mother—an alcoholic, chain smoker, depressive, cheated on my mother's father, abusive.

This is what I imagine:

My mother is four years old, and she finds a dying bird lying on hot concrete. Its wings and legs must be broken because it just lies there, flopping like a fish out of water. My mother, transfixed by it, watches until it makes its last flop. Then she pokes the bird's feathers with her fingertip; already her nails are bitten to nubs. When the bird doesn't move, she picks it up, one hand for its body, one to hold its head. To save the stiff, soft body from the sun, she brings it in to her mother, who is taking a bath.

Her mother's body looks unusually large and curvy, magnified by the water's surface. There is a hardness about her, too. She is a sunken gourd, the hollow inside swollen with water. Her knees peek through the surface, two bony turtles' shells.

What's most striking is her hair, the yellowest yellow you ever saw. Really her hair is darker like mine and my mother's. Years of nicotine have made this baby-doll, too-bright yellow.

When my mother brings her the bird, her palm opened for her mother to see, what she has in mind is to lay the bird body along the porcelain edge of the tub, like an offering. But before she can place it there, her mother splashes her and the bird and tells her to get out of the house.

"You have no sense," she yells.

My mother hides the bird under an empty, upside-down flower pot for later because her mother is already calling after her again. Her mother, naked except for a frayed lime green towel around her middle, knocks her on the head several times, each one harder, and tells her to scrub her hands.

"Thick, thick skull," she says. "Nothing but bone in there."

Minutes later, her mother emerges from her bedroom in a bright orange sleeveless dress, low cut in the front, a red scarf wrapped around her still-damp hair. My mother thinks she looks like an angry vegetable.

"Get your shoes on," her mother says, wrapping a pecan roll in brown paper and giving it to my mother to carry. This is when my mother is the youngest child, and her siblings are all in school.

My mother trails behind her mother. She watches the orange skirt hem fall behind and catch up with her mother's round, pink calves. Her mother does not ask her to hold her hand. She doesn't turn around to see if she is still there.

When they get to the man's house, her mother leaves her alone on a scratchy sofa. Her mother throws her arms around this man's neck, and he all but drags her away as if she is a bag of stolen goods that must be quickly hidden.

My mother stares at a painting of an owl on a tree limb. Its eyes are like two yellow moons with black holes.

Our Story

I return home from school to find *The Texas Chain Saw Massacre* on the kitchen counter, a fresh bottle of vodka next to it. *Texas Chainsaw* is our favorite. It's the triple-chocolate truffle of slasher films. When the Sawyer men place the hammer into shrunken old corpse-looking grandpa's hand and he keeps missing Sally's head, dropping the hammer like it was a pencil, you just can't help but smile. I mean it hurts so bad that if you don't smile, you'll cry.

Slasher films mean one of two things: either a really good day or a really bad day. Most often it's the latter.

"Know that Colleen woman I told you about?" my mother says when she comes out of the bathroom wearing a cream-colored robe, a purple towel wrapped around her head. The skin under her eyes is yellow. Her sinuses.

"Who?" I say.

"I came back from lunch today with a slice of cheesecake, and she had the nerve to roll her eyes at me. She said that I sure ate a lot and that there's just no way possible someone could eat so much and stay so small. I swear to you she was trying to say I must have one of those eating disorders, bulimia or something, or else I'd be fat like her and the rest of them in there. All of them are just plain jealous of me because I'm not fat. They're all just a bunch of miserable old cows."

"You're just the belle of the ball, Mom," I say. "Everyone knows it's lonely at the top."

"I just can't stand a single one of them. They're all so mean and hateful. It's hard to believe people can be so terrible." She rubs the towel against her hair.

"Not so hard," I say. I unscrew the top off the vodka, get a bottle of tonic from the pantry, and set out two glasses. I put three ice cubes in each, fill them halfway up with vodka, the rest tonic.

I pass her a glass.

"I worked hard to be where I am. I took night classes while working full-time and raising you, and all by myself."

"I know," I say. I show her a pizza from the freezer and wait for a nod, which she gives.

We put in *Texas Chainsaw* and each curl up in our own blankets at opposite ends of the couch. A few times our feet accidentally touch through the blankets, and we bounce off each other back into our curled-up, boxed-up houses. We're like mollusks or clams or conchs. We like being sucked up inside ourselves, safe in our own salty warmth.

The Terrible Place

I saw the house she grew up in just once. This was also the only time I ever saw my grandparents. My mother took me to visit them the Christmas before her father died. They'd found cancer in three different places in his body, so I guess she wanted to see him one last time.

The living room was like a place deep under the ground. Whenever I thought about being buried alive, usually I thought no oxygen, bones desperate for space, and the worst kind of aloneness you could imagine. But being buried alive with other people, your family, and the smell of them as they suck up oxygen that could have been yours: that was worse.

Three scrawny, hairless dogs were piled on top of each other in a round bed next to the television. The house smelled like hairless dog skin.

The rest of the house was closed doors with thick, mottled glass, so that all I could see were faint shadows. There was almost no light in the house except for in the kitchen.

My grandmother's hair was thin and yellow and half-hidden under a pale blue scarf. Her face seemed yellow too, and I could barely understand what she said. I remember that I asked my mother later whether my grandmother was from another country.

My mother said, "You can't understand her because she's smoked cigarettes her whole life. She's lucky she can make sounds at all."

The kitchen table, which was nothing more than a large card table, the kind my mother would erect so that we could put together a puzzle, was covered with sweets my grandmother had made. Metal pans were arranged like a mosaic. There were brownies, oatmeal cookies, butter cookies, a cake with cherries and marzipan, and fudge, peanut butter and chocolate. She pushed the pans toward me, and I hesitated. I knew the story of Hansel and Gretel. Maybe my grandmother wouldn't try to fatten me up to eat me, but something bad would surely happen. If I put those gruesome sweets into my mouth, my hair would fall out or I'd turn a dull, sickly green.

My mother didn't touch the food, so I felt I had to. I felt sorry for this woman, my grandmother, who seemed so small and whom my mother didn't touch or smile at. But I was afraid of her, too. My mother wouldn't treat her that way unless she'd done something awful. My mother held her father's hand. She asked him if he was taking care of himself. She brought him packages of summer sausage and a cheese log. She wasn't a bad daughter.

"I'm sure going to eat good," he said.

Before we left, my grandmother stood and lifted a cardboard box from the top of the refrigerator. She handed it to me, and I noticed that her nails were bitten down like my mother's. She said, "Merry Christmas," and I looked at my mother.

"Go ahead," she said, so I opened the box to find a little book with a faded orange cover, the spine barely holding on. It was called *Bitsy the Spider*.

"It was your mother's. I found it in the hall closet," my grandmother said.

In the car on the way home, my mother asked me if I really wanted to keep that old torn-up book. "We could go to the bookstore. I'll get you some nice, new books. I'll get you whatever you want."

"I want to keep it because it was yours," I said.

My mothers' dark blonde hair was tucked behind her ears, and her lips were pulled tight. She looked fierce, like she was going to tear up the road.

Our Story

It's a Friday night, and though we've hardly spoken all week, my mother comes home with a large gold plastic bag.

I'm making tea when she enters the door. She smiles at me.

"I got you a present," she says.

"A present? What for?"

She gives me a look that asks why I'm not playing along.

Earlier in the week I developed a rash on my stomach, and when I told her I was worried about it and wanted to see a doctor, she told me it was nothing and that it would go away.

"I don't think so," I said.

She said I was a hypochondriac—this from my mother, who is sick all the time.

I went to the doctor on my own, and it turned out I had scarlet fever. Within a couple of days, the rash covered most of my legs and arms and chest. They weren't little spots like hives. My rash was like a puddle of purple ink, spilled all over my body. I looked like a burn victim.

It was thirty degrees outside, but I walked around the house in shorts and a tank top, not just because I was burning up half the time, but because I wanted my mother to see my skin, to see what she had called hypochondria.

For three days I was in so much pain I couldn't sleep. No over-the-counter pain medication would do the job.

She hasn't said a thing to me, though. What she did was yesterday she brought home a bag full of soup packets.

Now there's this gold bag.

"Open it up," she says.

I'm scared to look. My mother's gifts are always disappointing, if not downright depressing. Inside the bag are two plain white boxes, and I lift the lids to find two wigs. Both are long and straight, but one is red and the other is blonde, a good deal lighter than mine or my mother's hair.

"You pick whichever one you want," she says.

"And you're keeping the other?" I say.

"That's what I was thinking, but if you want both of them, that's OK. Try one on."

"I don't know," I say.

"Come on. Put one on."

"Did they cost a lot?" I ask. This always makes her angry, but I hate to think of money wasted.

"No," she snaps. "They were a bargain. Why don't you try the red one?"

I lift the red wig from its box. It's longer than I realized, and it's the color of cinnamon. My hair is already up in a bun, so I slip it over my head. I haven't a clue how to do this. My mother adjusts it for me. She's grinning from ear to ear.

"Look in the bathroom mirror," she almost whispers.

I look like a stranger. The wig must be a pretty good one because I think that if I didn't know better, I wouldn't know it was a fake. I imagine myself running through the aisle of a drug store, knocking bottles from shelves. My lipstick is smeared across my cheek, and I am singing at the top of my lungs.

"I was thinking Sally," my mother says. She doesn't have to say *Texas Chainsaw*. There is no other Sally.

"But Sally is blonde," I say.

"I don't know. It's long and straight like hers. You could try the other one. It's blonde."

"But why should I want to be Sally?" I ask.

My mother cannot answer me. She is quiet, and then she says, "I'm so sick and tired of your mouth. I try to do something nice for you, and this is what I get."

"I like it," I say, and I think that perhaps I'm telling the truth. This girl fits my mood. I feel malicious. "It's pretty. It fits real well. Why don't you put yours on?"

"They'd both look better on you," she says, still agitated. "You keep them both."

"No," I say. "You always do that. I want you to put the other one on. It's yours."

"No, no."

"Yes. I'll help you."

I pin back her hair with a handful of bobby pins. I feel cruel somehow, my hands in her hair like this. Her hair is dry and brittle from years of coloring. The bobby pins give her the look of a woman who hangs out in laundromats, smoking cigarettes and coughing. My mother has never smoked a cigarette in her life, yet she has aged like a smoker. Stress has laid its hand on her. I set the blonde wig down upon her head. I pull and tug until it seems snug. She was right. It doesn't look good on her. The blonde is too blonde.

"Look at you. Now there's a Sally if I ever saw one," I say.

"It's heavy," she says.

"Yes, I know," I say.

"Do you think people get used to it?" she asks. She is running her fingers through the strands. It hurts me to see her do this.

"Somehow I don't think so," I say.

The Weapon

Words mostly, I think.

When I won a couple of awards at my junior high commencement, my mother told me she was proud of me. Then she told me I was lucky that I had someone who was proud of me. She said that she never had that.

"It's not like your mother wanted you to fail," I said. I didn't believe then that a parent could intentionally hurt her child. It's not that I never felt hurt by my mother. It's just that I believed she wanted the best for me. I never had any-one to compare us to. I didn't have anyone but my mother.

"She told me I was worthless," my mother said.

"She didn't use *that* word," I said.

"She used that very word. She said terrible, mean things to me. You can't begin to imagine how terrible a mother can be to her own children. You're lucky. You have a good mother who works hard for you, and who loves you."

And I remember thinking, but what about all the times she called me a jerk? If it's terrible to call your child worth-less, is *jerk* harmless?

And once my mother called me a "fucking bastard," but that was an accident. My mother almost never swears. She believes that swearing is one of the surest ways to tell if someone's trashy. On the rare occasions when I've let foul words slip out of my mouth, my mother has let me know in no uncertain terms that talk like that will hold me back from everything worth wanting in life. Good-bye good job, good-bye respect, good-bye boyfriend or husband.

"I just want you to have a good life. My mother never did care what became of me," she said.

And I thought, what about her brothers and sisters? There are six of them. As far as I understand, they are all still in contact, with each other and her mother. It's my mother who left. She's the only one who ran away and never went back. She's the only one who escaped.

So, is she the only victim? Or the only survivor?

☾

Our Story

After putting on the wigs, we get drunker than we ever have before. Usually, we have just one or two vodka tonics, just enough to make us warm and tipsy. And even that is rare, maybe once or twice a month. My mother is adamant that we not "overdo it." This is so we don't become like her mother. If I start to pour more than two drinks, she tells me I better not become an alcoholic. "It's in your blood. Don't let it out," she'll say.

But in these wigs, we are not ourselves; or maybe we are more ourselves than ever. We drink, and we drink. We end up sitting on the apartment balcony. The chairs are covered in snow, which we knock off with our bare hands. We plop right down. I've changed into sweatpants and a sweater. I can no longer feel the aches in my tired, fever-ridden body. The vodka has numbed me. Instead I feel a dull ache in my head. My head is a dancer in a deranged music box. It spins and spins.

My mother holds the vodka in one hand, her glass in the other. She is slumped back, but her gaze is focused. In the long, too-blonde wig, she looks like a puppet or a mannequin.

She says, "Sometimes I really hate you. And then I have to stop myself and remember who you are and that you weren't sent here to eat me up."

I don't feel shocked by this confession. Somehow, this seems the most natural thing. It's like getting the dish on someone, and you just want more.

So I say, "Sometimes I really hate you, too." I can't feel my lips enough to know whether I'm grinning as wide as I think. I want this to go on all night. I want us to have it out until we're kissing each other on the mouth. There is a part of me that knows I probably won't feel so good about this in the morning, but for now I'm spinning with desire. It's like I'm all tentacles, a giant squid. Give me, give me, give me.

"I can't imagine how you could be more different from me. That's the problem. We're just so different," my mother says.

Oh no, I think. She's got it all wrong. We are the same, she and I. We are nearly identically flawed. And that's usually what I fear and hate the most. But for this one night, I love it all.

"We're the same, and you know it," I say.

"You don't even know how different," she says. She isn't looking at me. She's looking at the porch opposite ours. Every building in the complex is identical. The porch is strung with red Christmas lights, and the chairs are turned upside down to keep the snow off the seats.

"Oh, Mom," I say. I'm giddy. "You're so silly. We're not different. We can't talk, and we can't say sorry and love and—"

"No," she says, sharp this time.

"Let's just say it all, Mom. Please. Let's say everything," I say.

"Say what? I've told you. I hate you sometimes. And I shouldn't have told you that. You shouldn't know about that."

"But I do know. It's OK."

"I'm going to bed," she says.

Oh, God, all I want is for her to hold me. I want to tuck myself into her stomach and neck. And she could touch my hair and kiss my forehead and eyelids. I want to smell the salt on her. But none of this is going to happen.

I watch a bleach-blonde stranger fumble with the sliding door and hear her curse under her breath each time her fingers slip from the metal handle, leaving smudge marks on the glass. I watch her disappear into the apartment, the door snapping shut behind her.

I stay out there on the porch, and I see my mother running through brambles. Everything is gray and yellow. She is barefoot, and her hair is long like the wig, but real. There is blood on her face, and her eyes are big and wild. Her skin is scratched and torn. She isn't screaming, though. I can hear only her breathing, thick rasps in and out. And something is chasing her, a loud rumbling, but I can't see it. She throws large stones over her shoulders as she runs. She is taking the stones from under her ragged T-shirt. It's like she's pulling them out of her stomach. She's trying to kill or slow down whatever is chasing her, but the rumbling never stops. It's like an engine. It's a crunching, heavy noise. It makes her head swell, this noise, but she keeps running and throwing those stones.

With my mind, I try to reach into this picture and lift my mother out of it. I try to switch us. Let me run for a while, I think. I'm stronger than her, younger. But it's no use. It's that kind of dream, the kind you have no control over. Trying only wears me out. I know I better get myself inside. It's dangerous to pass out in the cold, and it must be twenty or below out here.

PROLOGUE

My mother was the girl who pushed the witch into the oven, only it wasn't quite like you've heard. She entered the witch's house alone. Her siblings—there were four of them—weren't survivors. When their parents left them by that fire deep in the woods, the first child climbed a tree and wrapped herself in a cocoon she would never emerge from; the second chopped wood for hours on end until, his vision blurry, he mistook his legs for logs and bled out in intricate rivulets; the third buried himself beside a poison ivy, and the ivy crept spider-like along the forest floor; the fourth submerged herself in a murmuring lagoon.

My mother wasn't fooled by the bread walls, the cake roof, the window panes made of sugar. She knew that sweetness was often a trick.

But always, she took what she could get.

You know what happened next. The witch took her in, gave her free rein of the pantry.

What you might not know is that life with the witch was not all bad. There was food aplenty; a warm, soft place to sleep. In the evenings, they sat by the hearth and told stories.

For her room and board, my mother had chores, and, yes, the witch was sometimes on her back. My mother kneaded the dough too roughly; she swept the floors too harshly;

she clanked the dishes too loudly. But, my mother conceded, the witch's criticisms were not unjust. My mother never was much of a homemaker.

This business about the oven, my mother didn't see it coming. Sure, the witch remarked on the fit of her clothes, the curves of her flesh. What woman didn't assess the bodies of the girls in her care? And the witch, she couldn't have been more lovely about it—never a cruel word, only flattery. It wasn't until the witch instructed her one day to stick her head inside the oven to check that it was hot that my mother gleaned she'd been duped. My mother nursed her broken heart by sucking severed pieces of sugar window pane while the witch's scream dwindled in the fire.

The part my mother didn't tell me, the part I know without a doubt to be true, is that she trusted no one thereafter. Yet she married and gave birth to a daughter of her own.

ALIEN EYE

Sam's coworker Carla is talking about her three-year-old son Rico's obsession with death. "He says to me, 'Mama, I don't want to die. I really, really don't want to die.'"

They're in the nail aisle of a Home Depot on the south side of Houston, counting nails. They've been in this aisle for hours. Some inventory specialists get antsy counting the same merchandise for long. When it's a big box store, those folks head straight for the big stuff—paints, planters, light fixtures, toilet seats.

Sam has no objection to staking out a spot on concrete flooring and emptying out bins of nails only to place the nails back into the bins in clumps of five. When it's nails he's counting he can easily count twenty or thirty thousand in a day. He likes to guess how many nails are in a bin before he counts it. He's remarkably good at this, within five percent almost every time.

Carla says, "I tell him I don't want to die, either. Sometimes I tell him I'm sorry he has to die someday. And you know what? I really am. In a way that hurts. Maybe it sounds dumb, but I feel like I've failed him somehow. Happy life, kid. While it lasts."

"That doesn't sound dumb," Sam says. He punches numbers into his counting machine. Only two percent over. His guesses are usually over rather than under. He places the finished bin back onto the shelf and pulls out another.

"Once I told him, 'Don't stress about it, Rico. Odds are you'll live to be a rickety old man.' He said then, 'But sometimes kids die, right?' Where does he get this stuff?" she says. The way she looks at him then, it's as if she expects him to provide the answer. He likes how she looks at him, like she's known him a long time, even though it's been just a few weeks. She's always nice to him, Carla.

She's only a few years older than Sam, but in terms of life events, she's like light years ahead of him. She's been married and divorced. She has a kid. None of this was planned. She'd been a teenager, seventeen, the age he is now, when she got pregnant. Now here she is counting inventory year-round, not just for the summer like him, to save up money for college in another year. She's been counting nails since before Sam got his driver's license. The way she talks, this is it.

"When I was a girl, I wanted to be a flight attendant," she once told him and a couple of other inventory specialists. They'd been counting bedpans and urinals at a medical supply store. "Not on an airplane, but on a rocket ship to the moon. I imagined myself floating through the aisle with a tray of astronaut ice cream and drinks in little pouches."

Counting inventory isn't all that bad. It involves mathematics, after all, and requires no handling of other people's food, which in Sam's mind puts it above being a flight attendant, even on a rocket ship to the moon. But still, the idea of Carla counting nails and bedpans until she dies disturbs him greatly. She never had a chance.

After they've been quiet for a while, Sam tells Carla about his mother's coworker dying at the office, about how his mother has been renewing her CPR certification all her adult life and never had an opportunity to put her skills to use and so here it was, finally, her chance to save a life, but it turned out this woman had the old-school fake boobs that stick straight out and don't budge and that they were ginormous, so his mother couldn't get close enough to the woman's heart to do chest compressions. "Can you imagine? Killed by your breast implants?"

Carla laughs. Then, "So, what's with that finger of yours?"

He sees that his left pinkie finger is arced away from his ring finger like a wishbone begging to be snapped. It's poised, watching. It used to be a conscious thing, *alien eye,* something he did only when he was alone. He extended his pinkie finger and reported facts he read, like people over the age of twelve view over four hours of television a day; or scenes he observed, like an elderly woman in a checkout lane at Sigmund's begging her middle-aged son for a chocolate bar, insisting, "But I've been a good girl!" But since he returned from a summer science and engineering camp in New Mexico, his finger has begun extending on its own without his realizing it. It's as if his finger is operated by a very remote control. He knows that's not really true. Aliens aren't sitting in front of a monitor far, far away, watching and listening to Sam's transmissions. He isn't really from another planet, as much as he may feel like it sometimes. It's just pretend, something he started up as a kid. Sam Cleave, ethnographer of humans. Alien spy.

"I broke my finger, a long time ago. It's been a little off ever since." He makes up the lie on the spot. Then he presses his pinkie back into alignment with the rest of his fingers.

☾

Summer camp was a devastating disappointment. First off, as a result of his father having been out of work going on eight months, his parents couldn't afford to send him to the six-week program he'd originally planned to attend. He'd had to settle for two weeks. Secondly, and most importantly, he'd thought that at camp he'd finally belong for the first time in his life, that he'd meet *his* kind of people, his *tribe*. All his life he'd been the smart kid, the red supergiant in a sky full of dwarfs. When SAT scores were reported, his physics teacher patted him on the back. "Highest score in the junior and senior classes combined! Better thank your parents for those genes!" Mr. Kinney said. Sam went off to camp thinking he could do anything he set his mind to and that for the first time in his life he would be surrounded by fellow supergiants and that in their presence he would thrive like he never had.

But at camp he realized he wasn't a supergiant after all. The other kids at camp had experiences conducting the kinds of research Sam had thought only people who had completed graduate school did. Many of them were children of scientists. Their parents taught at universities. These kids, they'd lived in other countries because of their parents' work. One kid had repeatedly visited the Large Hadron Collider as it was being constructed. More than one of them had sat at dinner tables with Nobel Prize winners, and they referred to these scientists by first names as if they were old friends. Whether these kids were smarter than him or just more fortunate, he didn't know, but what did it matter which it was? The fact of the matter was that he felt lonelier there than he had ever felt in his life. It was like he'd woken up to find that the sky was not blue but yellow, and it had always been yellow, and he had been the only person on the planet unable to see.

Sam watches Alex Atwater and his girlfriend, Janelle, drop eggs from an overpass crossing the Gulf Freeway. They've gone through two cartons and haven't come close. They time it all wrong, waiting until a vehicle is directly below them before launching.

"Here, you try," Alex says, thrusting a white-shelled chicken egg, the cheapest Sigmund's offered, into Sam's hand. The shell is strangely thick and rough like some doctored ingredient in the caged chickens' diets has led to a Hulk-like mutation.

Sam wants to tell Alex to fuck off. He's wanted to tell him that ever since he returned from summer camp to find that everything Alex does anymore is aimed at impressing Janelle. Before Sam left, Janelle didn't even exist, not in Sam's world anyhow. She was just a girl at school. But at the beginning of summer she became a girl with whom Alex spent five days a week in the mail room at the medical school in Galveston where they both work, and after Sam left town, a girl with whom he spent his evenings and weekends too.

This is Alex's second summer working in the mail room. Come fall after their graduation the next year, he will most likely still be working there. Alex has no plans for college.

Sam also wants to shame the two of them by pegging a vehicle on his first try. All night Janelle has treated him like something out of a Dr. Seuss book, something queer, to be marveled at.

Without knowing exact distances (i.e. from the egg to the ground, from the vehicle's current position to the spot directly below the egg) or the precise speed of the car, he cannot possibly do the math required to ensure that the egg and the vehicle collide, so it's a combination of estimation and instinct that guides him to drop the egg when he does. As the egg falls, it looks miniscule, harmless, but when it lands on the windshield of a white Lexus SUV, the vehicle swerves, jerks back into its lane, and then skids to a halt along the edge of the median.

The three of them are in Alex's pickup truck within seconds, the remaining eggs stashed quickly beneath the seat.

"Shit," Sam says again and again, while all the while Alex and Janelle hoot and holler.

"I didn't know you had it in you, Sammy," Janelle says. She slaps him on the knee.

"Shouldn't we drive faster?" Sam asks.

"You may be a good shot, but you know nothing about fleeing a crime scene," Alex says.

Alex is his oldest (and only) friend. If he knows anything about fleeing a crime scene, he learned it from Janelle this summer.

Alex parks in front of a late-night diner that serves just about everything—pizza, burgers, omelets, and most importantly, a roasted vegetable dish Sam has ordered a half-dozen times.

"Seriously?" Janelle says when he orders. She doesn't even wait for the waiter to disappear.

"You think eating animals that have lived miserable lives on factory farms gives you character?" Sam says.

"What the fuck?" she says, turning toward Alex, whose arm is wrapped so tightly around her neck that he barely has to turn his head to stick his tongue in her ear.

"Alex!" Janelle says.

When their food arrives, Janelle doesn't say anything, but she looks Sam in the eyes as she lunges at her burger. When she finishes chewing, her lips part, and she says, "Fucking delicious."

Sam's boat-length Oldsmobile groans whenever he applies the brakes, and in this way, he can be sure that his mother will know he is returning home at past two in the morning. His father is another story. A tree could crash through the roof, and as long as it doesn't rock the bed or crush his bones, Leonard will sleep right through it.

Leonard hasn't always been such a deep sleeper. After he lost his job the previous fall, he stayed up late seven nights a week watching movies. His eyes were rimmed red. He bumped into furniture. That lasted a little over two months until Sam's mother, Bonnie, decided that Leonard had been allowed more than enough time to wallow in self-pity. "Until you find something, maybe you could make use of this free time. Make dinner? Clean the house? Since you're here," she said.

Even without the car's signature groan, Bonnie would sense Sam's return. She seems to have some sort of telepathic power when it comes to Sam and his sister.

She is cool, however, his mother, or was, before she became the sole breadwinner for a family of four. When he burned a hole into the carpet in his bedroom during the construction of an elaborate Rube Goldberg machine back in junior high, she said, "Let's clear out some space in the garage for you." When he scorched a good cooking pot during a chemistry experiment, she said, "I trust you'll replace it." No scorn. No judgment.

These days she scans the house the second she comes home from work, looking for flaws. Sometimes she hasn't even taken her shoes off or put her bag down before she's launching complaints. The mail is on the kitchen counter, breakfast dishes on the dining table, piles of laundry on the couch. Exasperated, she pours herself a glass of wine. Look at her glass too long, and she'll say something like *I think I've earned it.*

What troubles Sam more deeply than anything his mother will think or say about his late homecoming is what she would think if she knew what he did a few hours earlier. The car didn't strike the median or another car, thank goodness. It didn't flip or turn circles or catch fire. But any of those things could have happened. He had known that, and he had done it anyway. It didn't matter in the least that he'd dropped only one egg, whereas Alex and Janelle had dropped a dozen each. It didn't matter that he'd been horrified, whereas Alex and Janelle had been delighted.

After little more than four hours of sleep, Sam climbs into the company van with Carla and several other inventory specialists. Their manager, Eddie Skeet, is the driver.

"Counting the biggest home improvement store in all of Houston today," Eddie says after he starts the van's engine. "You're going to count until your fingers bleed! Ha!" A woman in the middle row of the van is a question-asker: How many people will be working this store? When do we get our lunch break? What if we're not done before dinner? All I brought is lunch. The older gentleman seated in the passenger seat claims to have counted this store five times now. He claims to remember that the last time around, they finished the job in precisely ten hours and ten minutes and that he had a bag of Doritos and a packet of powdered donuts from the store's vending machine for his dinner. The question-asker lets everyone know that she will not touch anything from a vending machine even if it means she starves to death. "I don't think we'll be there long enough for anyone to starve to death!" Eddie says. "Ha!"

Carla says, "Man, Rico kicked me in the ribs all night long."

"That sucks," Sam says. He inhales the cinnamon molecules traveling from her mouth to his nose. He does not tell her about his own night.

"People say I should make him sleep in his own bed," Carla says. "But then I just lie awake all night listening and worrying. I think every tiny creak or groan is his window pane sliding open. I think some psycho is going to break in and take him away from me. I know it's crazy. I mean, god, listen to me. How did I turn into such a lunatic?"

"I'd probably be the same way if I had a kid," Sam says, and he's surprised to hear himself say it and equally surprised that perhaps there's some truth to it.

"For your sake, I sure hope not. It's sweet of you to say, though." Then, "I bet you'll make a good dad someday," Carla says. She smiles at him, and her eyes glitter.

"So, what's the story with Rico's dad?" Sam says. He looks at the seat back in front of him as he says it.

"The story is he's a loser," Carla says. "He's still living with his mom. He hasn't worked a job for more than two months straight in his life. He's too busy playing video games to bother with Rico."

"Sorry," Sam says.

Just then Eddie lays on the horn as a red pickup truck nearly smashes into their van.

"Texting," Eddie says. "That motherfucker was texting away."

"The average teenager sends 2,272 texts a month," Sam says, both to his coworkers and to his pinkie finger, which seems to have involuntarily poised itself like a hook to record.

Sam's father was sacked on a Friday, and the next evening they'd driven out to George Observatory in Brazos Bend State Park. Clearly Leonard had kept the news from Sam's mother, too, because she kept smiling at Sam and his sister, Evie, through the rearview mirror as she drove. "I've wanted to do this for years," she said. She reminded them of how she'd dreamed of being an astronaut when she was a kid, and how crushed she'd been when she realized how outlandish this dream was for someone like her—a girl, and a girl who grew up in a Podunk town in Texas no less, a girl whose parents never went to college.

"You two can be anything you want to be," she told them for like the thousandth time. "Don't you ever let anyone tell you you can't."

For Sam, there was little worse than hearing about his parent's disappointments and regrets. He said nothing, and neither did Evie.

Leonard said nothing, either, not a word the entire drive except when Bonnie asked him to help her find a particular exit, and he said about ten seconds later, "Your exit."

Their guide at the observatory was a young black man named Devon who made jokes that were only mildly funny, but at which Bonnie laughed with her whole body. When Devon took them outside, Earth had spun just enough that all that was visible of the sun was a faint peachy glow along the horizon like crumbs left after a meal. Soon the darkness swept over that, too, erasing the sun's traces clean away.

Leonard stood apart from the crowd, staring off to the east at the darkness Earth was spinning toward rather than the faint traces of light it was spinning away from.

Binoculars were passed around. Devon gave the group a short talk about what they could see through them. Then he returned to Bonnie's side.

Watching his mother with this man, Sam saw how she could have had a very different life. He could see plainly what she had missed out on, what she had given up. That's what he believed anyhow, that she'd traded her dreams in for Leonard, a man who didn't seem to have any dreams as far as Sam could tell. He watched movies and sports, went to the gym, and that was that.

Sam shivered. He found a spot away from the crowd and lay on the still-somewhat-warm concrete. He looked up at the stars with his naked eyes. They blinked on and off as though they were relaying messages in code.

Something strange happened to him then. As he stared straight up at all that glitter, he felt suddenly like he would fall off the planet and into that endless abyss. The sensation sent chills through his body. His fingers grasped stupidly at the rough concrete for something to hold onto.

What brought the sensation of gravity back was the sound of someone crying, a man. Sam turned on the tiny red light on his key fob and searched around the dark, and there he found Leonard holding on tight to the railing. Never had Sam heard his father cry. That those awful gooey sounds were coming from Leonard made Sam sit straight up and listen.

He thought his father was crying for his mother, that he had seen what Sam saw—a woman who had given up something vastly precious. This made him like his father more.

When he later learned the real reason his father had been crying, Sam felt like he'd been sucker-punched. It wasn't that he didn't feel bad for Leonard losing his job, but the realization that his father hadn't noticed his mother whatsoever that night, that her joy had completely escaped him, was a devastating blow. His parents had wasted their lives, he thought.

They're lying on freshly mowed grass along the edge of one of the many bayous that run in and around Houston. Courtesy of Janelle, Sam has just swallowed his first tablet of ecstasy. The sky is fading from indigo to black, and as it does so, new stars pop through. Their numbers are growing steadily now like pustules or hives in a case of dermatitis.

The grass feels plush as if it's a huge stuffed animal.

Sam says, "Force equals mass times acceleration. Momentum equals mass times velocity. Change in momentum equals mass times change in velocity. Change in momentum equals impulse. Or mass times change in velocity equals force times change in time." The way these equations all piece together makes him ridiculously happy.

"Good god," Janelle says.

"Kinetic energy equals mass times velocity squared divided by two."

"Alex, make him stop," she says.

"I can't make him stop, but I can make it so you don't care anymore what the heck comes out of his mouth," Alex says.

"Come on," Sam says. "Don't you hear the poetry? It's all connected. All you need are a couple of variables, and you can calculate the rest. With just a few details, you can solve for so much."

He's smiling with his whole body.

"God, has he always been like this? Put me out of my misery, babe," Janelle says.

"Good ole, Sam," Alex says and laughs.

Alex is lying closest to the slow-moving waters of the bayou, and Janelle curls toward him then and wraps her arm around his chest. Sam hears the rustling of the rearranging of limbs. He holds his arm up and arcs his finger so that it can record whatever it is that they're doing. He doesn't care at this moment if they see.

"Power equals work divided by time," he says.

Soon he feels the warmth of a hand. It's Janelle's hand. She is reaching behind her, pulling him toward her.

"Let's shut you up," she whispers.

When his body is soldered onto hers, she places his left hand onto her helmet of a hipbone. Other than Crystal Frisco in the seventh grade, the girl he had *gone with* for a grand sum of two days before she broke up with him, Sam has never touched a girl before. As he moves his hand back and forth over Janelle's hip, Sam thinks of Carla and of a tiny tadpole-like Rico swimming about a little pool between her hips. At about ten weeks' gestation humans look incredibly similar to the way most people imagine extraterrestrials. They have huge, bulbous brains that take up seventy-five percent of their heads; milky, glassy eyes like egg yolks without the albumen; and smooth faces with almost no features, no lines. Sam's extraterrestrials are no different.

This is what he's thinking about when he slips his pinkie finger inside the warm folds of Janelle's vagina. He wonders about the transmission the aliens are receiving. Does a tiny light blink on so that they can see? Does the light make the wetness glisten? He imagines a group of green heads huddled close together in front of a video monitor. The heads alternate back and forth from one shoulder to the other as they try to make out what it is that Sam is showing them.

Alex's hand bumps into Sam's arm as he cups Janelle's left breast. Alex's eyes are closed, but there can be no mistaking that he is cognizant of Sam's trespass. It occurs to Sam then that it is all Alex's idea, that he whispered something to Janelle, something like *Poor Sam. Will you let him feel you up? For me?* Alex would do a stupid thing like that for him. When Alex talks about the future, it's always set here, in the town where they grew up. The two of them are still hanging out. Their lives are still intertwined. The difference is they hang out in bars, they get laid a lot, and they don't have their parents to answer to.

Sam's plans for the future have never been a secret. It's just that Alex doesn't seem to recognize the conflict between their plans, that in order for his own vision of the future to come to fruition, Sam's vision would have to fizzle out.

Janelle stands up and announces she's going to go pee. She walks around to the other side of the truck. Sam can hear the stream of her urine searing the soil.

Alex says, "Have fun?" He is grinning from ear to ear.

"I feel kind of queasy actually. It must be the ecstasy," Sam says.

"What?!" Alex says. "Seemed to me like you were enjoying it."

When Janelle returns, she retrieves the half-gallon of orange juice from the cab of the truck and drinks straight from the mouth of the jug. She passes it to Alex.

Alex drinks, then passes the jug to Sam, and places his arm around Sam's neck. "I love you, man," he says, "even if you are fucking crazy." He rubs his other hand across the top of Sam's head.

Sam remembers how in the fifth grade the school carnival included a jar of jelly beans that you could win if your guess was closest to the actual number of jelly beans in the jar, and how Alex spent a ridiculous amount of time counting every jelly bean he could see. When he finally wrote down his guess, the teacher manning the table didn't put his slip of paper into the box as she had Sam's. She said, "Alex, that's all you're going to guess is in this huge jar?"

"I counted," Alex said.

"Bless your heart," the teacher said. "What about all the jelly beans in the middle that you can't see?"

Alex had said simply, "How am I supposed to count what I can't see?"

Sam had known even back then that Alex was not the kind of guy he would have chosen for his friend had he had a larger pool to choose from, but the fact was the pool was small in his little Texas town where the farthest anyone ever went was another Texas town.

But now that he has seen what is on the outside, he knows he doesn't belong anywhere on Earth. He is like some strange hybrid animal, a liger or a grolar bear or a wholphin. He isn't this or that. He has no tribe.

When he held the egg in the air over the Gulf Freeway, he thought about how its rough shell held, or did once, the ingredients for life, and how its fate was redirected not once but twice; and how in other parts of town right at that moment, other eggs' fates were being redirected at the doors and windows of houses.

That's how Sam feels, like a sterile egg careening toward the windshield of a moving vehicle.

When Alex and Janelle decide they want to hop into the truck and hit a fast food joint, Sam announces he's going to walk home.

Janelle gives him that Dr. Seuss look again, like he has feet sprouting from his head.

"I just feel like taking a walk," he says.

"A two-hour walk?" Alex says. "Sam, what's going on with you? Are you OK?"

"I just feel like being alone," Sam says.

"Hey," Alex says. "Don't just walk away like that. It's not cool, man."

"Sorry," Sam says. Then he turns away from them, just like that.

They're counting baby grooming supplies, little safety nail clippers and pastel brushes with bristles like silk, at a baby store, and Sam says, "We should hang out sometime."

"Like outside of work?" Carla asks. "Like go out for a beer?"

"I don't have a fake ID," he says. "But I could give you the money to buy us some beer. We could go somewhere, like a park maybe. Rico could come, too."

Carla grabs hold of a rack of finger toothbrushes so as not to lose her place. She studies him.

"Sam, I—"

"That rocket ship dream you told me about, Carla, I can make it happen," he says. Does he still believe this? Yes, he thinks. He has to. For Carla and Rico. Saving Carla and Rico is his one shot to make his life mean something.

"I'm going to be an engineer. I know I told you that, but

the thing is what I didn't tell you is that I plan to build the kind of rocket ship you talked about. Well, not exactly the same. It won't be a commercial ship. I'm not taking a bunch of assholes with mouths full of potato chips up into space with me. You won't be serving anybody anything. It can be just you, me, and Rico. We'll fly to the moon together. We'll travel farther than the moon. We'll go anywhere we want. We don't ever have to come back here."

"Oh, Sam," she says.

She glances at his finger. He snaps it back into place.

"I can do it," he says. "I know I can. I will."

"That's sweet, Sam, but that whole rocket ship thing, it was just pretend, when I was a kid. I didn't mean that I wished I could still do it. I don't want to fly to the moon."

"What?" he says. "Why not?"

"I have a life," she says. "Here."

"This?" he says.

"What do you mean?"

"Counting inventory?"

She looks away.

"You deserve more than this," he says.

There are tears in her eyes.

"I want to give you the whole universe," he says.

She turns back toward him.

"I don't want to be given anything," she says. "I take care of myself. I take care of Rico by myself. I do a good job."

He reaches out to touch her.

"No," Carla says. She holds the palm of her hand out like a stop sign.

On his walk home last night, he peered through living room window after living room window, where the people of his town sat in front of their televisions, their bodies like shed exoskeletons left behind on the furniture.

When he felt like he couldn't take anymore, he lay down on an area of the sidewalk where he could get a clear view of the sky, unbroken by trees. He looked up and waited to fall off the planet. He arced out his pinkie finger while tears tart as lemons welled up in his eyes. *Please come and get me, please*, he thought, but the stars chattered away as though he weren't there, as though they didn't speak the same language.

LIKE PULLING TEETH

In the kitchen, the girl's parents told gruesome stories: children's teeth lassoed to doorknobs, pickup trucks, and the tails of family dogs. The removal of baby teeth was an extreme sport. Cheese sounded kind in comparison, until the girl saw its blue-green crevices and sniffed an odor that also suggested crevices.

"Won't it just fall out on its own?" the girl asked.

"It's more fun this way," her father said. He'd voted to tie her tooth to the ceiling fan.

"You said it was bothering you. The quicker you get it out, the better. Like a cactus spine," her mother said, as though the girl's tooth were a foreign object.

After, staked in the stinky cheese, her tooth looked as strange as a flag in the cratered surface of the moon.

Her parents said, "This is a big milestone for you. You're growing up."

Up, the girl thought. Growing up was a process of coming undone, like a seam slowly unraveling. One tooth down, nineteen to go. In her nightmares, they all fell out at once.

When the girl had learned that kids' teeth fell out, she'd thought that eyeballs, fingers, and entire limbs were cast off and remade, too. That children regenerated themselves piece by piece, like lizards replacing severed tails, until nothing of their child bodies was left: That's how they became adults.

Her father had laughed and said, "No, no, that's not how it works." Then he'd gotten quiet for a moment and said, "Well, actually, maybe growing up is a little like that."

Her mother had told her about elephant teeth, how they got six sets instead of two. Because they wore them down like pencil erasers. "Now the final set, they're something! Eight pounds apiece!" her mother had said.

"That's the permanent set?" the girl had asked.

"Well, no, not necessarily. They can fall out too, eventually. If the elephant lives long enough."

"Then what?"

"Then the elephant starves to death."

A boy from the girl's preschool class had died that past year. Choked on a hot dog, there at the lunch table. Their teacher had wrapped her arms around his chest and pumped, but the hot dog hadn't come out. The girl thought of the boy when she chewed. How death had been in his mouth. How he could have spit it out if only he'd known.

This tooth wasn't the first part of the girl to die. Skin cells died too—every day, by the millions. Her mother scrubbed them from her feet with a gray stone, and they formed a dusky pile resembling sawdust. And hairs came out in her brush—long, soft hairs that snaked in and out between the bristles. Her father left stubby, gray-black hairs in the bathroom sink. They looked like tiny punctuation marks shaken from a slip of paper.

Always the body was regenerating itself. Always it was dying.

But a tooth: that was something else. Like a button pop-ping off a blouse. There was a gap now. She was incomplete.

Her parents pinched parts of the cheese wedge that held her tooth and put them into their mouths. Their jaws moved up and down like pistons.

They talked about the fairy that was going to purchase her tooth in the night—snatch it from beneath her pillow and leave in its place coins.

"How much does the fairy pay for a tooth?" the girl asked.

"I used to get two dollars," her mother said.

"Rich girl," her father said. "I got fifty cents."

"Fifty cents?!" the girl said.

She imagined the fairy, that cheap creep, dancing around a fire, children's teeth jangling from his ears and neck.

Now her mother yanked the tooth from the cheese. She held it up to the light, as though inspecting a gemstone. "My baby's first lost tooth," she said.

"It isn't lost," the girl said. "In fact, I don't think I'm going to sell it."

Her parents stared. "What are you going to do with it?"

The girl plucked the tooth from her mother's fingers. In her palm, it looked like something that might wash up on an ocean shore, and the girl thought now, for the first time, how what she'd collected in her pail that sum-mer were the remains of the dead. How she'd been like the tooth fairy of the beach, skipping along the sand and snatching up carcasses.

This new keepsake was a promise that she would one day die, too. That death was in her mouth, all the time, and there was no spitting it out. Perhaps that was why people yanked baby teeth out by wild means, when everyone knew the teeth would fall out on their own anyhow: They wanted to believe that great effort was required to fall apart. That it wasn't a simple matter of waiting.

HOW MANY WAYS
CAN YOU DIE ON A BUS?

None of us knew any kids who'd died on a bus, but that's because by the time we started riding, people were more informed. They took precautions. Deaths were becoming more and more rare.

But we could rest assured that children still managed to find new ways to die on buses. We had to be careful. We had to be smart. That's what Lucy, our bus driver, told us. Lucy was strict about the bus rules and had an endless supply of them, too. Just when we began to relax again, Lucy would tell us a new story of death and disaster.

In the beginning, it was pretty simple. We had to stay seated while the bus was moving. If we were standing, we might fall. Or worse, if the bus crashed, our bodies might turn into little torpedoes. We might shoot out the front window like the Fourth of July. Children had been known to do just that. They shot out windows and knocked their skulls hard on glass or tar or concrete, and they died. Sometimes on contact. Other times they lay in hospital beds for weeks before death took them in its thick, hairy arms.

Of course, we shouldn't eat or drink on the bus, either. Partly, this was to keep the bus clean, and surely we could understand that, Lucy said.

Her crimped orange hair whipped into a wave, pouring from one side of her head and spilling onto the other. She said, "Heaven knows I'm not you kids' maid or your mother."

We could attest to that. Lucy was nothing like our mothers. She wore pink eye makeup, and her nails glittered gold. When a car didn't stop behind the bus so she could let us off safely, she hollered out the window. "Child killers! Nothing but a bunch of murderers!"

The only thing Lucy had in common with our mothers is that she wore a golden cross pendant on a chain around her neck. Hers was a little larger than the crosses our mothers wore or that some of us wore. We figured this meant Lucy was real serious about the Lord.

The other reason we shouldn't eat or drink on the bus, Lucy told us, was that it was not unheard of for children to choke to death on buses. If Miss Lucy had to hit the brakes just a little bit hard to avoid hitting a chipmunk or a squirrel, a lollipop could not only lodge itself in our throats so that we couldn't breathe, it could puncture something back there. We could have to eat our meals through tubes in our stomachs. If the lollipop stick was positioned at just the right angle, it could poke up into our brains. We could lose our speech or our sight or muscle coordination. Or we could die.

Then there was the warning that horrified those of us with long hair, girls mostly. We could not hang any body parts out the window, especially our heads. We should, in fact, make sure that not the least bit of our hair got caught up in that exhilarating wind rushing past the windows. We should tie it back if needed. Or else it could get caught in a passing tree limb, and no matter how loud we screamed it would be too late. It would be impossible for Lucy to stop the bus in time to save our heads. The hair would be ripped from our scalps, probably with our skin too. We would be scalped. We might not die, but what would that matter if we had terrible heads that no one wanted to look at?

Then Lucy began making us show her our backpacks when we got on the bus, so she could be sure everything was zipped up.

"And keep them that way," she said. "No taking out notebooks, rulers, and especially not pencils or pens or compasses."

We could not only kill ourselves but each other with these items. A boy in Oregon had been holding a pencil when his bus crashed into a van, and the pencil punctured the flesh of the girl sitting next to him and went straight through to her heart.

"And what do you think happened?" Lucy asked us.

"She died," we said.

"Damn right, she did. And I don't want no children dying on my bus. You hear?"

"We hear."

Before we knew it, Lucy suggested that if we were tall we should sit low in the seats so that our heads didn't reach above the seat backs.

"What about our postures?" we asked.

"Do you want to deal with bad posture or do you want your head to swing back so far that you can't ever pull it upright again?"

You have to realize that Lucy wasn't trying to be mean. She believed everything she told us. And there was such worry in her eyes and voice when she issued these warnings that we believed, too.

We stopped having any fun at all on the bus. We sat still, our heads against the seats, our bags zipped, our lunches sealed shut, and we found ourselves with nothing left to say. Before, we had sung songs and told jokes, but none of that seemed appropriate anymore. Our songs and our jokes were dirty, and they were mean. They were about women having sex with repairmen and bakers. They were about men peeping into holes to watch women pee. They were about how retarded people have sex. They were about how Siamese twins have sex. They were about girls named Texas being stabbed deep in their hearts.

On the bus, we were conscious of how fragile we were. Life could be taken from us quickly and in the most absurd and embarrassing ways. This was not a time to joke about how a man or woman without hands masturbates. We didn't want to push our fates. On the bus, we pretended to be good little children. We were quiet, and we thought only good thoughts. We thought about how much we loved our mothers and fathers, and even our siblings. We thought about how we would start working harder in school. We thought about how we would never steal or cheat again, if we just made it off the bus alive. Some of us prayed.

Then came Prue Hildeman. She was a scrawny little thing with mousy brown curls and red-framed glasses. She had a big dimple smack dab in the center of her chin. Her first day on the bus she brought a Walkman. Lucy asked her to kindly put it in her bag and to never bring it on the bus again.

"You could be strangled in the cord," Lucy said, and we nodded.

Prue looked at Lucy and us like we all had toes growing out of our ears.

"That's got to be the nuttiest thing I ever heard," she said.

"No kid has ever died on my bus, and I won't have you coming on here and changing that," Lucy said. "Put that thing in your bag."

"What a psycho," Prue said as she settled into a seat in the back row of the bus.

"Be quiet," we said.

We had to turn to look at her. We didn't sit all the way in the back anymore. The back of the bus was for telling jokes and propping feet up on the seat backs. The back was for smuggling on potato chips and sodas.

Prue rolled her eyes. She put on her headphones and danced in her seat to music we couldn't hear.

We thought we heard Lucy growling under her breath, and this worried us. We didn't want Lucy to be upset. All she did was look out for our safety.

We didn't like Prue. She was trouble.

"Sit still," we said.

"Hey," she said, her arm dangling out her window. "Did anyone hear the one about the prostitute and the corn farmer?"

"Heard it," we said. "Keep your body inside the bus. Quiet now."

"I'm going to kill my parents for moving here," Prue said to herself, but loud enough for us to hear.

We sucked in our collective breath and closed our eyes, as if to dissociate ourselves from her. If we couldn't see her, we couldn't be accountable for her devilish acts. Whatever she did, we were innocent and would not be punished.

"You idiots," Prue said again and again. "I can't believe what a dumb old town full of dumb old people this place is."

We thought, she'll see who the idiot is when she bites it right here on the bus. She'll be sorry when she's lying in her grave, when she has maggots feeding on her eyeballs and tongue.

But some of us couldn't take our eyes off Prue. She broke every rule on the bus. She chewed on Sugar Daddies. She drank fake fruit drinks with straws sharp as cats' claws. She ate meats on sticks. She did jumping jacks in the bus aisles, which wasn't only a threat to her own safety, but it was distracting to Lucy, and it was a fire hazard. She sat on her knees to make her head loom over the seat. She hung her whole head out the window and screamed in the wind so that her voice spread out like a ricochet.

And there seemed to be nothing Lucy could do about it. She spoke to Prue again and again. She told her the very stories she'd told us. She told Prue she thought she would have a nervous breakdown.

And we thought that maybe she already had. Lucy was letting herself go. Whereas before, the glittery polish on her nails had always been perfect, not a chip in sight, now she went for days without touching up the tips. She was no longer taking the time to crimp her orange hair either. It was frizzy and unbrushed, and it seemed to be accumulating some gray. We thought we saw gray in her brown eyebrows, too.

It wasn't just her appearance. Lucy took sharper turns. She screeched at stop signs. She took the Lord's name in vain.

It got so bad that if we wore crosses around our necks, we rubbed them and prayed, making all sorts of promises. Those of us who didn't wear crosses crossed our fingers. We wanted to live long enough to get our driver's licenses. We wanted to survive long enough to find out what sex was really like. We wanted to move out of our parents' houses and live in swank apartments in big cities. We wanted to have sex on penthouse balconies. We wanted to make lots of money and be famous. We hoped that these were legitimate wishes and that we weren't jinxing ourselves as much as Prue was jinxing us.

However, after a month or so of being called dumb by a bouncy, rule-breaking, healthy-as-ever Prue, we started to *feel* dumb. Maybe she was right. Perhaps it was nutty to think we would die if we told our dirty jokes or if we dangled a hand out the window every now and then. And what were the chances we would die from sucking on some candy? We couldn't all die of these things, right? And if one of us did die, as a kind of sacrifice or message to the rest of us, it would probably be some kid on the other end of the bus, a kid we didn't know too well.

Slowly, we began to relax. We didn't act as crazy as Prue, but we broke our silence at least. We started telling jokes again. And it turned out we knew jokes Prue hadn't heard before, and that was real satisfying. When Prue threw her crazy, curly head back and laughed at our jokes, we felt good. We felt clever, even though we hadn't made up the jokes ourselves.

It wasn't long before we were violating all of Lucy's rules. When the jokes didn't kill us, it seemed logical that the other things probably wouldn't either. We dangled a few fingers out the window, then entire hands, then arms up to the elbows. We sat up again, not worried about what would happen to our heads now that they had no seat backs to catch them if Lucy had to slam on the brakes.

Lucy responded to our disloyalty with emotional pleas. She announced that she could see our chips and our Cokes and our dangling arms and that this hurt her immensely.

She said, "You children are not only making me a nervous wreck, you're breaking my heart. Where are your hearts? Do you children have hearts?"

We said we were sorry, and we shrunk down into our seats so that she wouldn't have to see what upset her so. It wasn't our intention to hurt her. Truly, we loved Lucy. We loved her like we loved our mothers. We figured that just as our mothers understood our kind of love, Lucy must, too, even if she seemed not to.

The fact was we couldn't return to the old way of doing things. We'd broken Lucy's rules, and what she'd said would happen hadn't. We were still alive, and it felt good. We hated to see Lucy upset, but all we could do was shrug. Lucy was wrong, if not a bit crazy. She'd tried to put the fear of God into us, and it had worked for a while. But we saw through all that now, and perhaps for the first time ever, we made up our own jokes. We whispered jokes about crazy Lucy. How crazy is Lucy? She's so crazy she thinks B.O. stands for brain odor, so instead of smelling her armpits she taps the side of her head to see if anything is leaking.

Lucy stopped talking to us, stopped checking our bags and telling us when she saw us breaking rules. Sometimes she even forgot a kid's stop, and we all had to yell at her.

She looked as if she hadn't slept in weeks. She looked as if she'd seen a whole busload of ghosts. She had bags under her eyes, and she sometimes forgot to zip up her bus driver pants. It wasn't pretty.

We talked about what we might do to make her feel better. One kid suggested we get a dollar each from our parents and buy Lucy some flowers or chocolates.

"You know, girly stuff," he said. "We could make it anonymous. We could write on the card, *From your secret lover.*"

"Where would we send it?" a girl asked.

"To the bus barn," the boy answered.

"That's so conventional," another girl said. If we wanted her to feel special, we needed to do something more unique.

"Like a cookie bouquet," somebody said.

"No," the girl said. "Like an origami lantern or a pretty scarf to tie up her hair."

Then we found out that one kid's grandma pickled all kinds of vegetables and cross-stitched little lids to go on top of the jars. She sold them at a market, but he thought he could get us a few jars for free. That settled it. Pickled vegetables it was.

Another kid's mother kept around a big box of gift bags and bows, so she agreed to bring the wrappings for the jars. The two kids would sneak these things onto the bus, and we'd put it all together on the way to school. Another of us agreed to make a card that we would all sign. We were all in on it. Prue even volunteered to give up some Sugar Daddies to include in the package.

We had to do a lot of seat changing that morning because everyone wanted to see the gift and sign the card without Lucy seeing what we'd gotten her. We knew how much our moving around the bus upset her, so we tried to be quick about it. And anyhow, we figured she would forget all about it once she received her gift.

The kid with the grandmother who pickled things had managed to get us three jars—one of cucumbers, one of baby corns, and another of tiny pearl onions that looked like colorless eyeballs. The jars were big, as long as three of our fists in a line, and wide too. The stitching on top of the jars was of a cat napping, a little church with a steeple on top, and the third said, "Ho Ho Ho! Merry Christmas!"

When everyone had signed the card with their names, and some with messages like "Stay cool!" and "You're the most kick-ass bus driver ever," the kid who'd brought the red gift bag and gold string put the card in the bag with the jars and secured the string into a bow around the bag's handles. It was ready, and we all settled down and were quiet. We thought about how thoughtful we were, how sweet. We smiled in anticipation of the moment we presented our gifts to Lucy. We imagined grateful tears rolling down her face.

Then an unexpected thing happened. The kid sitting next to the girl holding our gift, unprompted by any slam on the brakes or sharp turn, began choking. He'd been sucking on a Jolly Rancher.

In his panic he flailed his arms and knocked the girl with the gift hard in the chest. His blow must have knocked the air out of her. The girl dropped the gift. Those of us near enough saw the bag fall as if in slow motion. Everyone heard the shattering of the glass as the jars hit the floor of the bus. We quickly lifted our feet so that the liquid and vegetables wouldn't get on our shoes. The stench hit our noses. We struggled to get our windows down. We screamed for Lucy to save the choking kid.

She pulled the bus to the side of the road, and she ran to the back where the kid was choking. She jumped over a couple of puddles where the pickled juices had leaked into the aisle. She grabbed hold of the boy and squeezed him hard under his ribs. Out of his throat flew a green piece of hard candy about the size of a dime. It stuck to the back of the seat in front of him.

Lucy stood in the aisle and stared at us.

Then she said, "I intend to write up every single one of you."

One kid explained to Lucy that we had gotten her a gift, that we had been trying to do something special for her.

Lucy eyed us suspiciously. "Pickles?" she said. "What would I want with pickles? Would any of you want pickled vegetables?"

Perhaps not, we thought, but everyone knew it was the thought that counted. Her making fun of our gift was simply rude and ungrateful.

"And what could you have been thinking to bring glass onto my bus? Do you know how dangerous that is? What do you think would have happened if that glass had flown into one of your faces? You kids aren't responsible enough to ride on the bus. I am going to make sure that you kids aren't allowed to ride a bus for years to come, not until you learn how to behave on one. And if your parents can't drive you to school, I guess you'll just have to walk."

We were shocked. Lucy had never threatened to write us up. She had never said anything about kicking us off the bus. Our parents would be angry with us. We would be punished. We couldn't let her do it.

A kid in the back stood up and announced that her father was a superintendent of the school system and that if Lucy so much as tried to write us up, she would make sure that Lucy lost her job. She said she was willing to make up stories about Lucy's bad driving if she had to. She would tell her father that Lucy drank while she drove. "I don't want to do this," the girl said. "I like you. We all like you. But if you make us, we will report bad stories about you. Right everybody?"

We nodded our heads and breathed sighs of relief.

Another kid said. "We have nothing against you, but you just can't get us into trouble like that. You don't know our parents."

We really did feel awful about all that we had put Lucy through, but we couldn't let her kick us off the school bus. That was going too far. We would do whatever we had to. It was a matter of survival.

Lucy looked really sad and kind of scared. "You children would try to put me out of a job? You'd make up lies about me?"

We lowered our eyes.

By the time we looked up, she had turned around and was walking toward the front. Then she opened the door and exited the bus.

We hung out the bus's windows and watched her walk north up Dover Street. We watched in silence as Lucy's body became so small we couldn't see her anymore, not even a dot of her. We sat there helpless, unsure of what to do. We were at least a couple miles from school, and if we were going to get off the bus and walk, we certainly didn't see the point in walking to school of all places. We might as well walk to the mall and see a show and eat pizza and ice cream. But none of us could move.

Eventually the cops found us and took us to school in squad cars, four and five to a car. They explained to our teachers that our tardiness was to be excused because our bus driver had abandoned us in the middle of town. Throughout the day, all the other kids in school wanted to hear the story, and so we told them about crazy Lucy and how she had gone nuts and left the bus in the middle of Dover Street. We had known she was crazy, we told them, but we didn't know it would go this far. We told them about her rules and how she said there were hundreds of ways kids could die on a bus. We told them about her hair and her nails and her unzipped pants. We told them that a number of times we'd heard her mumbling to herself and that some of us thought she might have an imaginary friend. We told them about how she smelled of pickled vegetables. The story of crazy Lucy became legendary in our school. By the end of the day, every kid and teacher in school had heard all about her.

And when we told our parents what had happened, they hugged us hard and thanked God we were alive. They said that such an irresponsible woman should be put in prison.

To protect ourselves and make up for all the wrong we'd done, we followed Lucy's rules for a whole month even though our new bus driver, Jerry, couldn't care less what we did. We sat low in our seats, even Prue. We kept our body parts inside the bus. We folded our hands on our laps. We were quiet. We thought about how sorry we were and how much we hoped Lucy was OK. Those of us who prayed, as well as those of us who didn't, asked for forgiveness. And most of all, we hoped that what we'd done to Lucy didn't kill us or ruin the futures we'd planned out for ourselves. We hoped we would still make it out of that town to those swank apartments in the city, that we would be rich and famous and beautiful and have lots of sex.

SEX ED.

Mr. Platt handed out the babies like he was delivering grade assignments.

"Colic," he said to Tori, setting a plump rubber doll onto her desk facedown.

"Jaundice," he said to Marissa. Her baby had skin like my cousin Fiona who went on a carrot juice diet and ended up at a hospital where doctors force girls to eat.

Jem got croup, and me, I got "high needs." Our babies were the color of raw chicken.

"Me or the baby?" I asked.

"Both, most likely. Could be you consumed alcohol while you were pregnant. Could be you worried too much. Bottom line is your baby may be more demanding than some of the others," he said.

Then he passed around pamphlets from our federal government: *How to Care for Your Newborn.*

"Just the basics," Mr. Platt said. "You'll need to supplement your reading according to your baby's condition."

He informed us that our babies were sophisticated pieces of machinery. Not only were they each programmed to exhibit the symptoms of the conditions we'd been assigned, but they were able to detect and record a swath of data, from how often we fed them to the ambient temperature, to the force with which we handled them. The babies would know if we didn't give them the particular care they required. Mr. Platt would know.

He warned also that if we dared open the little compartments on our babies' backs to mess with the hardware, the babies would report that, too, and we'd receive zeroes on the baby assignment.

"Now, who can tell me what the most common reason babies cry is?" he said.

"Hunger?" Tori said.

Mr. Platt looked at us, inviting additional guesses.

"Dirty diapers?" someone else said.

"Gas?"

Mr. Platt just stood there, grinning.

"Is there a right answer?" I said.

"Nope," he said. "Half the time you won't figure out why the heck they're crying. Could be they're frightened by that pimple on your forehead. Could be simply that being a baby is ghastly: You're at the complete mercy of giants who don't understand you." He shrugged.

Tori spent nearly the entire week in the school cafeteria, rocking and humming and cursing. She was excused from classes on account of the colic. Jem and Marissa and me and Tori's boyfriend, JoJo, visited her from time to time. JoJo rubbed Tori's shoulders.

Marissa said, "Get a room."

Jem smirked. "Is that how you think babies are made?"

Me, I wondered what Tori's secret was. She and JoJo had been dating for six and a half months. Before that, it was Ben Gallop: four months. And before Ben, it was Nate Tagg: five and a quarter months.

The most prolonged relationship I'd had, if you could call it that, was with Ward Pitts that past summer. June and July he fucked me off and on, when his parents were out of the house. Then in August, just before school started up, he said, "This isn't a thing, you know."

JoJo was a year ahead of us and had been through this baby shit already. When Tori whined that she couldn't possibly take another minute, he said, "It's only a week. You'll get through it."

When she asked him to take her baby for her for a little while so she could get a break, he said, "Hells no. I've done my time."

"Fuck," Tori said to us. "Fuck. Fuck. Fuck."

"That's what got you into this mess in the first place," Jem said.

Marissa, who slathered herself in sunscreen (uncoated, non-nano zinc oxide only) and shielded her head in a floppy sunhat if she was going to be exposed to sunlight for more than a few minutes, took her baby outside between class periods. Sunlight supposedly broke down the excess bilirubin in the bloodstream, which was what had given her baby its pus-colored hue.

Her baby wasn't the only one who was rosy-cheeked at the beginning of every class.

"Forget your hat?" Jem said.

Marissa shrugged. "At first, yeah. But the sun feels kinda good."

Jem reported making her bathroom at home into a steam room by running a hot shower with the door closed. This was to moisturize her baby's breathing passages. Add a few plants and she'd have a rainforest, Jem said.

She complained about not being able to smoke cigarettes.

"Even if the baby can't detect cigarette smoke, Mr. Platt will," Jem said. "And I can't afford another failing grade in this class."

I wore my baby in a sling I made by tying two scarves together. Inside the sling where no one could see, I pulled my tank top down low, so she could nestle her head against my breasts. Skin-to-skin contact, that's what the books in the birth section of the bookstore prescribed.

My baby wasn't like Tori's, inconsolable no matter what. As long as she was in contact with my body, she was quiet. Put her down, and she wailed. That first shower, I didn't even rinse the conditioner out of my hair. I rushed to her, naked and dripping.

The babies were more life-like than you might think. True, they couldn't move their limbs and when you gave them a bottle, their mouths didn't suckle. But strapped against my chest throughout the school day, she felt as alive as any other being, with all those circuits and sensors monitoring me all the time. She was always paying attention.

At night, I wrapped my arms around her protectively as though someone might try to steal her in my sleep. Mr. Platt's pamphlet advised against "co-sleeping," but the books in the bookstore called this "attachment parenting." They said sleeping with your baby makes her feel secure.

I could understand that. Those few times Ward hadn't kicked me out as soon as he'd pulled his dick out of me, I'd watched him while he slept. The window air conditioning unit above his headboard had rattled, and I'd pressed my lips against his hot skin and arranged his arm around me and imagined he was my boyfriend. When a boy was out cold like that, you could fool yourself into believing anything.

☾

It happened Wednesday night.

The next morning, I nuzzled her and kissed her cheek, and it was like running my fingers across Ward's chest when he was asleep, like caressing a mannequin, only Ward's skin had always been warm.

I knew for sure when I stepped into the shower. She didn't make the slightest protest.

Mr. Platt said, "You slept with the baby, didn't you?"

"She cries if I don't hold her. The books said—"

"Cried. Past tense. She's dead now. SIDS. You probably smothered her in your sleep."

He took the baby away from me.

"You can't very well go around carrying a dead baby," he said.

In exchange, he gave me a new assignment: planning the baby's funeral.

While I calculated funeral costs, Tori, Marissa, and Jem decorated their babies. Tori puttied purple rhinestones to her baby's ears. Marissa wrapped her baby's bottom in a green cloth diaper she borrowed from her toddler brother's stash. Jem made her baby a black tulle skirt and a black pleather jacket with several zippers, much like the one she wore even though October in the desert was all sun and scorched earth.

They gave their babies daddies.

Tori chose JoJo, of course.

We sat outside at the picnic table under the school's largest mesquite tree. Its dropped pods crackled beneath our feet.

"Girl, you better watch what you say. You could be carrying his baby for reals right this minute," Jem said. She bit into a fried cheese stick from the cafeteria.

"Nah, I wrap that shit," Tori said. She picked at her slice of pizza. She complained about the grease.

Marissa, whose lunch was the same as always, a cucumber sandwich and a green apple, chose Paul Lambert, the same boy she'd had a crush on since third grade. We winced a little. If he so much as asked to borrow a pen, she stiffened and went mute.

Jem chose Justin Timberlake.

Me, I stared out across the school courtyard, where Ward Pitts stood at one end of a lunch table that wasn't mine. He bent his long body across the top of the table to snatch fries from Amanda Portsmouth's lunch tray. On the basketball court that summer, where he'd once smiled at me in that wink-y way he was smiling at Amanda now, his jump shot had lifted him so high into the air, he'd loomed over the bodies of the other boys like he was another species.

"What about you, Sammy?" Marissa said.

The soft cry that had been coming from Tori's baby grew exponentially now, and she shook the baby like she was making ice cream in a Ziplock bag, the way we had in chemistry class a few weeks earlier.

"I don't have a baby anymore," I said.

When Ward said that what we had wasn't a thing, I'd just gotten done tracing my face with the underside of the tip of his penis, like he was a blind man and I was trying to help him see me. I'd read in a magazine that that was the most sensitive part of the male body.

I'd said to him, "Nobody has to know."

I'd thought that if I could keep him around just a little bit longer, I might figure out what he needed, that getting Ward to love me would have been like figuring out why a baby was crying: If I just kept trying different fixes, something would eventually work.

But he'd looked at me like I was the sorriest dog in the shelter, the one missing a leg and wearing a cone collar and shaved down to the skin because of heat sores.

Now, Tori said, "Dead or not, it had a daddy."

I tore my paper lunch sack into strips. I didn't touch the peanut-butter-and-honey sandwich.

"Or do you think you're the fucking Virgin Mary?" Jem said.

The three of them laughed.

In the bookstore, I walked past the birth section and on toward the death section, where I inspected book after book about grieving.

A guy with a tiny conch shell hanging from a piece of twine around his neck joined me.

"Sorry you're grieving," he said.

"Sorry you're grieving," I said.

"My dog," he said. "Had her six years." He showed me a photograph of himself and a Saint Bernard. The dog's head was nearly twice as big as his.

"How about you? Who'd you lose?" he said.

I felt like I'd come down from a sorry attempt at a jump shot and had plummeted into the earth. Like I was wedged in concrete.

I opened my mouth to answer him, but my words, they were stuck in concrete, too. The only sound that could wriggle free was a howl from somewhere deep in my belly.

IF YOU WERE A SERIAL KILLER

A woman from my lab confessed at happy hour that she sometimes wishes her husband would meet an untimely demise while he's traveling for work. If she were to leave him, she fears she'd go running back to him. But if he were to die, well.

I tell Marina this while I repaint the kitchen walls. The red I chose the first time around, which is supposed to stimulate appetite, makes me feel as though I'm wedged inside the throat of a much larger animal.

I say, "This is what happens when people aren't honest with each other."

It's been two weeks since I put it to her bluntly: I'm not in love with her anymore. Nothing I said before seemed to jolt.

Initially, she looked as though she were in a state of cataplexy like the orexin/ataxin-3 transgenic mice in my lab. I give them leftovers from meals, and the more aggressive among them buck their more passive kin to get at the special treat. After, all of the mice lay motionless, impotent on the floors of their cages, the only sign of life the slow thumping of their furry chests. The excitement triggers a temporary, wakeful paralysis.

Like human narcoleptics, the mice eventually shake the paralysis off, and so did Marina, at which point she said,

"I've been stressed out. I've been worried about everything going to hell in the world. I'll make it up to you; you'll see."

Then came anger. She said I was cruel. She said I was insensitive. Heartless. Ruthless. Sadistic. She said, "I'm not one of your lab mice, Lori. You can't poke and prod me to see what will happen."

Now she says, "I'm not sure I like what happens when said people are honest."

I say nothing.

Marina stands at the edge of our kitchen, our sleeping daughter in her arms, and she stares at the living room furniture. I rearranged it the weekend before when I came home from the nursery with a ficus tree in a fifteen-gallon pot.

She says, "I'm never going to get used to this."

That's what I thought when I painted the kitchen red, but I gave the color a fair shake. Five years.

This time around I'm painting the walls green, first white to dilute the red, which Marina once said made her want to dance. For a week or so after the paint dried, she shimmied to the table with plates as her partners. That was a long time ago. Later, she accused me of choosing red just for shock value. "Like that damn Serial Killer game you used to play with your friends."

After this project is completed, I have plenty more lined up. I'm going to scrub the grout between the tiles with a toothbrush. Replace all the broken doorstops. Empty out every drawer and cabinet in the house and throw away everything that has sat idle for a year or longer.

"This is me not giving up," I say as I motion all around. "I want to fall in love with you again. I want this to work. But it won't if we're not honest."

She tries to smile. Her pain, naked and shimmering, makes her new again like an insect wriggling out of its pupal case, and I wonder as I dip the paint brush into the stark white if maybe I do feel something like love.

There's a pinworm infestation at Gretchen's daycare. All parents are encouraged to check their children for the parasites. They come out at night when the child's asleep, like Santa, the Easter Bunny, and the Tooth Fairy.

"Let's just assume she has them, give her the medication, and call it a day," Marina says.

When she was pregnant (she was adamant that it be her: "It's the most intimate one can ever be with another human," she'd said), she was vigilant about what substances passed into our daughter's body. She eyed deli meat with the disdain of a vegan. But now that we've entered the world of parasites—lice, nematodes, mites—she's quick on the draw with toxic chemicals.

I put on latex gloves and grab the masking tape. I hand her a flashlight and say, "You either help or I turn on the ceiling light."

As I sit on the edge of the bed, Gretchen rolls over onto her belly, cooperative even in her sleep. Nothing wakes her, not pulling her pajamas and underwear down, not even prying her cheeks apart. This is disconcerting but hilarious, too. My belly hurts with the effort not to laugh. I turn to Marina, wanting to share this with her. The flashlight is all that meets me. Marina's head is turned, and her eyes are closed.

☾

Marina comes home with two grocery bags full of vintage magazines and photographs.

"Doesn't it break your heart?" she says, holding up a black-and-white image of a big-eyed boy wearing huge chaps made of thick animal fur. It's like an exquisite corpse image—boy on top, guinea pig on bottom. He's hugging a small bird against his rib cage.

The walls of Marina's home office are covered with these old photographs of strangers. Not photos of us, mind you. Those are relegated to the rest of the house. Her office is a museum of lives that are not ours, of lives that have long since passed.

She plays curator to our relationship, too. When I point out problems—how we don't have fun anymore, for instance—she holds up dusty memories and says, "But look at how much fun we used to have!"

But her clutter is what drew a pack rat into our home when Gretchen was a baby. The animal made its presence known by chewing straight through her computer cord in two places, and as I discovered posthumously, it used the wires to line its nest. I set traps with bananas and cheese for five nights straight before I caught the animal. Each night before its capture it made away with the bait, leaving behind only tufts of fur, the fourth night a flap of skin the width of a dropper.

"Poor thing," she said. Her aversion to pests doesn't extend to mammals.

"That poor thing could have made us terribly sick. They carry diseases," I said.

"I know, but I still feel bad for it."

I, on the other hand, would have ripped that animal apart from limb to limb if it had come near our daughter.

"*This* is what breaks my heart," I say now, scanning the bags and boxes stacked wall to wall in her office.

What she does is not hoarding, she says for the hundredth time. Hoarders are empty and clogged at once, full to the brim with what's useless.

When our daughter runs through the doorway, Marina lifts her up and swings her through the air, and Gretchen yells, "Whee, whee, whee!"

"See, *this* is how I feel," Marina says. "Not empty. Not clogged." But I think that if I were to flick her with my nail, her face would crack.

Eventually, Marina pries loose her own disappointments. She sits across the dining table from me, amidst a backdrop of green. Like a dung beetle on a forest floor, she rolls shit into a gargantuan ball.

I encourage her. "Good," I say. "More."

After a while, her body droops. She says, "I don't want to do this anymore."

"It's good to get these things out in the open," I say.

"Good for whom?"

"Relationships are hard. Pretending that's not true doesn't make it any easier."

I tell her about Joseph Priestley's photosynthesis experiments, how he sealed mice inside glass containers with the company of plants. The oxygen was thin, but it was enough provided they didn't fling themselves against the glass.

"There's pleasure in surrender," I say. "Sometimes it feels like love. Sometimes it feels like death."

"You and your damn honesty," she says. "At least your coworker does her partner the courtesy of keeping her shit to herself. He's better off for it."

She's said the same thing about infidelity. She'd rather I lie than confess. She values preserving the illusion of cleanliness. But me, I'd prefer to be mucked up with the truth. I'd rather be with a cheater than a liar.

I say, "This is the great divide between us, but talking about it is good, see? Being open and honest makes me feel close to you again."

She smiles sadly and says, "You don't feel like you're suffocating?"

"Not right now," I say. I shrug.

I don't tell her about Priestley's control mice. Her mind doesn't go there on its own. But how else would he have discovered photosynthesis?

When the vacuum salesman shows up on our doorstep, I don't hesitate to let him in despite that the hard muscles in his arms shimmer as he hauls into our house a thick cardboard box, large enough to hold a body. He could snap my neck if he wanted to. He could snuff the life out of me with his two hands.

What he does is he removes a laminated photograph of a dust mite from a white three-ring binder and hands it to me. The creature looks like a scrotum that has grown legs and mandibles.

He tells me that allergy to dust mites is the most prevalent illness in the country. "If you're human, you're allergic to dust," he says. "We're all sick from it."

He claims that a mattress doubles in weight every five years from the accumulation of dust mites, skin cells, and dust mite feces. Whether or not his figures are accurate, our mattress is certainly heavy with the weight of us. It holds eight years' worth of discarded skin cells—eight years' worth of refuse.

When he vacuums a small swath of my side of the mattress, I watch through a window as soot-like particles pile inside the vacuum's cavity. "You see that?" he says when he turns the machine off. The way he points to the dust collected in there, like a doctor sharing the results of a diagnostic test, it seems indicative of some malady of my character.

He says humans shed about eight pounds of skin cells a year. I do the math: eight pounds multiplied by two people multiplied by eight years is 128 pounds of skin cells.

My coworker who thinks she can be rid of her husband if he would just die is wrong. Particles from his body would rattle around inside her chest forever.

When I send the salesman away, I lie back against the bed and breathe deeply. Pleasure in surrender, pleasure in surrender, I tell myself.

"Let's play Serial Killer," Marina says one night. Gretchen is asleep, and we're drinking beer.

I look at her skeptically. "Is there something you want to talk about?"

"I want to play Serial Killer. I go first."

"OK."

She doesn't have to think. Her answer is already planned out. She says, "If you were a serial killer, you'd break your victims' necks with your own two hands, decapitate them with a machete, then string their heads from a high ceiling like disco balls. You'd give them a spin and watch them whirl and splatter, making the room over into a Jackson Pollock. The bodies you'd have no use for. You'd dump them into the bayou in black plastic garbage bags."

Now I'm the one who's stunned. I can't twitch a muscle. I can't take my eyes off her. When I'm able, I say, "I think that's enough of that game."

"It's your turn."

"I pass."

"When did you become so sensitive?" she says.

Gretchen comes home from daycare with a clementine, woody flower buds of clove inserted into its flesh like eyes. She says to us, "Bacteria get in through the holes. You'll die if you eat it."

"Maybe, maybe not," Marina says. "What if we had nothing but this clementine to eat?"

"Then you would eat it first," she says to Marina. "If you live, Mom and I will know it's safe to eat. If you die, we'll know it's not safe to eat."

"Why Mama, Honey?" I say. I glance at Marina sideways.

"You're the tallest," she says to Marina.

Marina isn't offended. She smiles. She says, "That's right. I would eat the clementine first."

I can't leave it at that, though. Later, when our daughter's playing in the backyard, I say, "What if you couldn't eat the clementine first? What if it had to be her or me? Who would you choose?"

It's a ridiculous question. Of course, I want her to choose me to eat it. I just want to know what she'll say.

"Why couldn't it be me?" she says.

"I don't know. Let's say you don't have a mouth."

"I'm trying to picture this," she says. "This not having a mouth. Would my face be skin where my mouth is supposed to be? Would I have teeth in there?"

"Yes, you'd have teeth, and they'd be perfectly pristine locked away in your face, no contact with sugars and starches."

"Wouldn't I die?"

"You'd eat through a tube in your stomach."

"So I'm receiving food through my stomach, but you two have nothing but this rotten clementine?"

"That's right. Who would you choose?"

"I have hands, right?"

"Sure."

"Then I'd grab the clementine, and I'd get rid of it. I'd prevent you both from eating it. And I'd take the tube out of my stomach, and I'd give it to you two to receive nourishment from. I would pass it back and forth between you."

"You're not playing along," I say.

"You don't get to make up all the rules," she says. "Anyway, this mess about me having no mouth is plain silliness. We both know that my eating the clementine makes the most sense."

"How's that? Because you're the tallest?" I say.

We smile at one another.

"Because all three of us would choose me to eat it first."

"Oh, I don't know about that," I say, but I hesitate.

"It has nothing to do with love. We're just different in this way. I'd sacrifice myself first. You would not. You would for her, but not for me. And that's OK. I'm perfectly OK with that."

I look away. I say, "Well, you'd sacrifice yourself for a stranger on the highway."

"That's right. I would," she says.

This is how Marina makes her kills: she slips her arm around you from behind and presses her lips against your neck; the knife goes in clean and quiet.

UNIT 7: EXPLORING FOSSILS

Lesson 1: Engage

Denise tapped the side of the coffee tin with a boning knife to disperse the Plaster of Paris powder into the water. She stirred the mixture gently with a wooden dowel, careful to prevent air bubbles. What she ignored was the instruction to wear a dust mask over her nose and mouth. What with the vitamins she no longer bothered to take and the wine she no longer limited, what was a little particulate matter?

Garrick sat at the opposite end of their dining table, grading papers. He said, "This kid Josh wrote his essay about his older brother getting his driver's license. This he calls history?"

Once the Plaster of Paris reached a smooth consistency, Denise worked fast. It would set in minutes. She coated a nautilus shell and three clam shells in petroleum jelly and pressed them hard into the thick paste. The process was not unlike her mother shoving her two top front teeth back into her gums when she almost lost them at age twelve: she landed face first upon falling off her bicycle. It hurt like fuck, but thanks to her mother's pluck, the teeth had rerooted.

"History is history," Denise said. "There's no minimum age requirement."

"I gave them examples: The Vietnam War, the Great Depression, the Selma to Montgomery marches, Nine-Eleven."

"So the problem isn't the timing so much as the choice of event? Not worldly enough?" she said.

She coughed. A drop of urine leaked from her bladder.

"The problem is both. I told them to talk to their grandparents, and if that wasn't possible, then the oldest human they could find. I don't care what Josh's seventeen-year-old brother thinks about anything—getting his driver's license or the abduction of all those Nigerian schoolgirls, for that matter."

Denise stared at Garrick.

"What?" he said.

Sometimes she experienced a thrill imagining herself saying terrible things to Garrick, like "Maybe we lost the baby for a reason."

Instead she said, "Those girls are kids, too. You think they don't have stories worth telling?"

"All I mean is I don't think Josh's brother has a story worth telling. Anyway, recent history wasn't on the menu," Garrick said.

Denise tapped at the plaster to check whether it was dry. She pried the plainest of the clam shells first. "Isn't that how history is best preserved? By accounts from when the event happened?"

Garrick looked down at the stack of student papers on his lap. He spoke carefully. "That wasn't the assignment. The point is this kid wrote about his brother getting a driver's license, for fuck's sake."

Denise shrugged. "If I were in your class, I'd write about recent history, too. I wouldn't give a shit what grade you assigned me."

Garrick sighed. "Believe me, I know."

Lesson 2: Explore

Denise passed the plaster seashell molds around to the children.

She said, "These are mold fossils. Can anyone tell me how mold fossils form?"

"When bones or shells get pressed into clay," one of the children said.

"Good," Denise said. "Fossils are rarely the actual remains of organisms. Most of the time, they're just traces of that organism. Like a footprint or a mold or a petrified bone."

Or photographs, she thought: her stillborn child in the blue and taupe striped beanie and white gown Denise had received as shower gifts. The nurse had helped Denise curl her child's cold fingers around one of her own. "Someday, you will treasure this," the nurse had said, and Denise had turned and vomited into a wastebasket.

Or the flesh around Denise's belly and thighs that had yet to recede.

Or ghost stirrings in that belly that made Denise think she was pregnant again even though she hadn't had sex in well over three months, not since before she went into labor. Thirty-nine weeks: no reason to suspect anything was wrong.

Or the terrible words she *had* spoken to Garrick, like "Don't touch me."

Denise gestured toward the plastic tubs of dirt on the floor along the front of the classroom. She told the children they were going to conduct their own fossil hunt. "You're going to take turns playing three roles: excavator, archivist, and curator. The excavator digs carefully to locate fossils. The archivist maps the location of the fossil, removes the fossil, and cleans it. The curator records observations of the fossil."

She knelt on the floor of the classroom and brushed gently at the sediment in one of the tubs with a medium-sized paintbrush, to demonstrate. "You have to be gentle or you could destroy the fossils. Just because you don't see anything yet doesn't mean you're not close."

The night before, as she'd hid the fossils in the tubs like Easter eggs, Garrick had smiled sadly.

"What if we do destroy one?" one of the children asked.

"Just try not to," Denise said.

"But what if we do? By accident?"

"I don't understand the question," Denise said.

"What happens if a fossil gets destroyed?"

"Then it gets destroyed," Denise said.

"But then what?"

"Then you move on," Denise said.

"But does the curator record a destroyed fossil?"

"Oh, I see," Denise said. "Yes. The curator records everything."

Lesson 3: Explain

"Now we try to draw conclusions based on what we've found," Denise told the children. "What do we know about the animals that left these fossils behind?"

"They were small," one of the children said.

"OK. What else?"

"They suffocated?" said another child.

"What?" Denise said.

"When they were pressed into the sediment."

"Oh, no," Denise said. "They were dead before that happened."

"How did they die?"

"I don't know," Denise said. "We know the animals in the La Brea Tar Pits died because they became trapped in the tar. But most of the time, cause of death is a mystery."

The children stared at her the way Garrick had at the doctor, after the tests were run. "How can you not know how this happened? What are we supposed to do? Just try again and hope all goes well?"

Denise said now, "What can these fossils show us about how the environment changed over time?"

"It used to be covered in water," one of the children said.

"Good. How do you know?"

"Because the deepest fossils are seashells."

"And then what happened? How did the area change?"

"The water dried up?" another child said.

"Yes," Denise said. "Environments are always changing, as a result of earth processes such as erosion and weathering and deposition. It happens slowly, over thousands of years. What was once a sea can become a desert."

Lesson 4: Expand

"What's all that?" Garrick asked.

"We're going to build a scale model of *Troodon formosus,*" Denise said. She'd accumulated wire, cardboard, duct tape, glue, and a crate of other odds and ends for the project.

"What's the objective?"

She told him about reading to the children about Benjamin Waterhouse Hawkins, the Victorian artist who was the first person to build life-size models of dinosaurs, for the Crystal Palace.

"It was the children's idea," she said. "To better appreciate the size of these animals and what they looked like. *Troodon* is relatively small as far as dinosaurs go, but a good deal larger than the children. Actually, it leads us nicely into the next unit: adaptations. We'll get a close look at *Troodon's* anatomy."

Garrick shook his head.

"What?" she said.

In her home office closet, she kept a bag of flour. She'd scooped out white powder until the bag was exactly six pounds, one ounce. She paced around the room with it some nights, her eyes closed, the door locked. Garrick had commented a couple of times in bed that she smelled like bread, but that was the extent of his observations. He didn't ask questions. He didn't brush away the sediments to see what was underneath.

"Nothing," he said now.

He turned on the news. It was about the nearly three hundred girls and women the Nigerian military had rescued from Boko Haram. None of the schoolgirls who'd been abducted the year before were among the rescued. Not one, the reporter said.

Garrick quickly turned off the television. He closed his eyes.

Denise remembered something she'd read in the literature the counselor had given them, how the survival of any relationship, no matter its trials, no matter its history, boiled down to one thing: You had to lean into each other. The advice sounded so simple, but as she considered how to respond to Garrick—how to touch him, what to say—what she felt was the force of her mother's hand on her teeth.

RATTLESNAKE ROUNDUP

Ray was irritable during the drive up to Sweetwater, kept removing his baseball cap from his head and shaking it as though to dislodge a sticker burr.

"State your grievance," Tess said from the passenger seat of the motor home as they left Houston. She watched her husband carefully.

The kids were in back, both insulated by earbuds.

Ray said, "This weekend is about Dad. Why the hell would Mom do something like this?"

"Bring a date?" Tess said.

She was savoring Ray's misery, and there was nothing he could say about it.

They were caravanning to Sweetwater, Texas, for the largest rattlesnake roundup in the country to release Tess's father-in-law's ash remains. For three years, Ray and his sisters Joyce and Trudy had asked their mother what she planned to do with Cash's ashes, and Lynette had said she didn't want to talk about it. She hadn't approved of Cash's wish to get cremated. For that and other grievances, her kids had worried she'd kept him in that recycled peanut jar tucked behind spare toilet paper rolls as punishment. Then, finally, she'd said it was time.

The roundup had been Cash's affair. While he'd never collected thousands of pounds the way the top contributors did (that's how the Jaycees, who hosted the event, paid for the snakes: by the pound), every year he'd brought in about a hundred pounds or so.

Nobody questioned Lynette's decision about *where*. Considering they'd been asking her *when* for three years, they couldn't very well object to the timing either, except insofar as her unexpected traveling companion was concerned.

He was almost stilt-walker tall, and he wore black leather pants and a T-shirt featuring a fanged human skull. Add to that his devilish black goatee, thin mustache, and shiny black hair, and he resembled one of the shadowy figures from the covers of the trashy romance novels Lynette sometimes read.

Twenty-six to Lynette's seventy. He was a dark cabaret musician—stage name: Enigma. He'd produced two albums: *Wet-Feathered Feeling* and *Miss Muffit Under the Tuffet*. Vampires, cannibals, and ghost lovers who sucked the brains out of your head while you were sleeping were his subject matter. All this Tess learned from the Internet on the drive up after Lynette introduced them all to him in the parking lot of a Walmart where they'd met to caravan to Sweetwater together, three trailers and a motor home. It was a bold move.

Before Walmart, Tess had been the gruff traveling companion. Ray had been out of work five months, no unemployment checks on account of his resigning from his position as radiation safety technician at the hospital's request out of fear that the situation could become a lot worse if he didn't. The story Ray told his family was that another employee had framed him for something he didn't do. His eldest sister Joyce's response to that had been to say, "Well, if they all die of radiation poisoning over there, serves 'em right." What his family didn't know was that the employee in question had been a summer intern and that what she accused Ray of was making her uncomfortable by talking about his "marital dissatisfaction," this while offering her shoulder rubs. Withholding these details had been Ray's idea. He'd begged Tess not to tell them, this despite swearing up and down that it had all been a misunderstanding and that he'd most certainly not been hitting on the young woman. "You know me!" he'd said.

He wouldn't have told Tess either probably if he hadn't been certain she would find out from her friend Nevia, who worked in HR.

Ray made a wrong turn upon entering Sweetwater. He drove the motor home past ramshackle houses that Tess initially presumed were abandoned, so many of them had boarded-up windows, but then she saw a pair of cats feeding from a dish set along a door stoop. Further down the street, a dog dragged what looked like a T-bone, the meat long gone.

Recently, a sixteen-year-old girl had gone missing from the town Tess and Ray and all his family lived in. The girl's car was found abandoned alongside the highway just before the exit for the main road through town, the girl's purse and car keys on the passenger seat. Everyone believed this was proof she'd been abducted and probably they were right, but Tess wondered what details, like the cat dish and the T-bone, may have been overlooked. She wondered if the girl might have staged the whole thing. Once life got going on a certain course, it was difficult to change that course without taking drastic measures.

Tess said nothing about the unintended detour now, and she observed this as if from a distance. They were just two people traveling together along a road neither of them had seen coming. They were on an adventure. That was one way to look at it. Dr. Olive would see it another way. "When you avoid your feelings, the feelings don't go away. They're there under the surface still doing their damage. Like a boil. You need to get the crud to come to the surface."

Despite having never met him, Dr. Olive seemed to think Tess should leave Ray. She'd never said this directly, but every week at their appointment she pressed Tess to focus on what she needed and wanted, and to forget everybody else. There were questions she urged Tess to answer, questions such as if her relationship with Ray were a story she could write any way she desired, how would she write it? What did she dare not hope for? These questions had bored into Tess like the larvae of bot flies. She could feel them wriggling around beneath her skin.

Tess's head spun for hours, sometimes days, after her appointments with Dr. Olive. Like being a member of a cult was the analogy that came to mind, only she wasn't sure whether her counselor was deprogramming her or initiating her.

Tess's friend Nevia had been in and out of counseling for a couple of decades. She said, "That's because that doctor is taking a jackhammer to your snow globe. It feels scary, but trust me, it's a good thing."

Then again, Tess had long suspected Nevia didn't think Ray was good enough for her. After all, not even Coach bags or Godiva chocolates, things regular people would consider indulgences, were good enough for Nevia.

☾

A fat rattlesnake in the demonstration pit curled up like a house cat within inches of Tess's feet, only a transparent thermoplastic barrier between them. Its meek pose was betrayed by the sharp, black slits in its eyes, its lean snout, and taut body. Its glistening tongue, which poked out here and there to smell her, looked like the tail of some pitiful amphibious creature the snake was teasing, letting loose its throat's grip only to suck the creature back in again.

The man in the demonstration pit stirred the snakes that had collected together like helpings of spaghetti, the reverse of the Halloween prank Tess had pulled when the kids were little, shoving their small hands inside a cardboard box that concealed a heap of cold ricotta-stuffed manicotti. The man explained to the crowd that he had to move the snakes around from time to time so they didn't suffocate each other.

Ray, the kids, and Tess's in-laws were outside the coliseum eating sausages on sticks. They'd seen enough, or at least Ray had.

Within the couple of minutes he'd spent in the coliseum, his sullenness had morphed into anger the way it had the previous summer when she'd lured him into an art gallery to watch a performance artist cut a Texas flag into her chest with a razor blade as she stood naked before her audience and sang "The Yellow Rose of Texas." Ray hadn't cared what statement the artist was making. He'd said the whole thing was perverse. To make a statement of his own, he'd slept that night curled up in the back seat of his car, which resulted in a couple hundred dollars' worth of chiropractic adjustments.

The man in the demonstration pit had gentle blue-gray eyes, a color one might liken to a crystalline body of water, though the bodies of water Tess had known her whole life, the Gulf of Mexico and countless alligator-infested bayous and swamps, were brown or murky green. He wore a crisp white shirt and white Stetson hat and spoke softly about the importance of understanding the snakes. He said things like "When the sun has set the air on fire, I don't need my Kevlar boots. The snakes don't like that harsh sun. But when the temperature gets to around fifty at night and seventy or eighty during the day, that's when they're out looking for food, water, and companionship. They won't go out of their way to strike, but if I startle them, they will. They do it out of fear. They do it to protect themselves. I know this from living with them."

The majority of the Jaycees weren't so charming. "We stretch 'em and sex 'em, stretch 'em and sex 'em," a Jaycee in the weighing pit said in answer to Tess's question about what he learned by poking the snakes' tails with a metal probe. A Jaycee in the milking pit taunted her with a snake's pried-open mouth, like a school boy with a shiny new pocketknife. "Ah, come on. Give him some love." A Jaycee in the skinning pit spat out chewing tobacco as he slit a snake open along the length of its body, which hung from a hook above him. His bare arms were ribboned with tattoos of blue-skinned women, their hair fanning out as though they were under water, as though they had drowned, every last one.

The man in the demonstration pit pulled a yellow balloon from his shirt pocket and blew air into it. He rubbed the balloon up and down his body. To give it his scent, he said, though he'd told his audience that pit vipers sense their prey via infrared radiation.

The snakes hardly seemed to notice him. They lay placid as sunbathers. The only hint otherwise was the steady rattle that permeated the coliseum. The rattling hum seemed to come from everywhere and nowhere all at once as though Tess were situated inside the belly of it. When the man in the demonstration pit managed to gather a snake he'd been fishing for with a hooked metal rod and lift it onto the table at the pit's center, the animal's tail shot up like an antenna, but she perceived no audible change.

The first time he prodded the snake with the balloon, Tess shuddered. This was how some religious fanatics got themselves killed. It was the sort of thing she could imagine her father-in-law, Cash, doing, only the man in the demonstration pit didn't seem the least bit smug or cruel about it. He was nothing like Cash, who'd taken pleasure in riling people, as well as snakes. Sometimes Tess had gotten a kick out of watching him, especially when it was Ray's sister Joyce he was after. But he'd worn on her, too. He'd made the kids cry, sent Ray into depressions that lasted weeks.

The man in the demonstration pit circled the snake, and the animal rotated to keep tabs on him. They were partners in a strange dance. While he intentionally aggravated the snake, it was true, there was nothing cruel about the performance. There was softness in his movements.

Finally, after what seemed like several minutes of taunting, the snake had had enough, and it struck and popped the balloon.

The man didn't flinch. He left the snake on top of the table. He stirred the snakes in the spaghetti heaps. He said, "What I'm trying to teach you is that rattlesnakes are not aggressive creatures. The only time they're generally dangerous is in September when the females are caring for their young. Then they'll kill you. Outside of that, they're passive. They just want to be left alone. Leave them alone, and they won't go out of their way to strike."

Lynette's boyfriend circled round the demonstration pit then and stood next to Tess. He didn't say a word, but even so, she felt as though he were absorbing her with some kind of extrasensory perception, as though he were "seeing" through her skin and skull and into the folds of her brain, as if he could read her synapses. This is how she felt under Dr. Olive's gaze, too. Like they were playing Blind Man's Bluff, except Dr. Olive's card was tucked away in her palm; Dr. Olive could see Tess's card and her own, but Tess could see nothing.

The previous year Tess had visited the world's quietest room, the anechoic chamber at Orfield Laboratories in Minneapolis, for a magazine article she'd written about the science of sound. She'd heard her blood moving through her brain and heart, the tiny firings of her auditory nerves, and squeaks along the joints connecting the bones in her skull. She hadn't lasted five minutes. After, she'd staggered to the toilet and hung her head between her legs for fifteen minutes before she felt her body was in sync enough to manage the task of maneuvering down a hallway without bumping into something.

Lately she'd suffered similarly disorienting bouts. She was tuning into background noises she hadn't known were there.

Once when she awoke in the middle of the night to use the toilet, she was so startled by her own reflection that a curdling scream issued from her larynx. It seemed to ricochet through her, leaving a long hollow in its wake. She

hadn't recognized her own voice. This, more than the unan-
ticipated movement in the mirror, was what haunted her.
It had not been the scream of someone young and vibrant.
She'd pictured a stiff white nightgown that buttoned up
to the neck, a lonely old woman afraid of her own shadow.
When had she become the sort of a person who could produce such a sound?

Being the incredibly deep sleeper he is, Ray hadn't
heard, thank goodness. In the morning when she'd told
him about it, he'd said, "Everybody sounds like an idiot
when they scream."

He was wrong, though. Ray hadn't known her when she
was a teenager. Then she'd been a beautiful screamer. Tess
and her friends, Cath and Kiki, used to take turns. The idea
had been to imagine they were running from a psycho killer.
The girl whose turn it was closed her eyes and imagined herself alone with the killer, and when she was ready, she opened
her mouth and let sound rip from her throat like a hurricane.

Sometimes a psycho killer wasn't enough. Sometimes
they had to taunt each other to get there, like when it was
Cath's turn, they would pinch the fat along her bra strap
and say she was as plump as a biscuit and that the killer
was going to slice her open and butter her up. When it was
Kiki's turn, they chastised her for having been so desperate for a boyfriend that she let Skip Nolan plant hickeys
all over her neck during lunch break at the Burger Basket.
When it was Tess's turn, Cath and Kiki went off on her
crazy bitch of a mother and how she better hope she didn't
end up like her, alone and angry and pathetic.

Always, always, when the screamer got there, when the
fear penetrated the lacquered kernel of her core and shat-
tered her from the inside as it burst forth through her

throat, they all three knew it at once. They all three felt it. After, they collapsed, exhausted, a pile of sweaty limbs and smeared mascara. Except for the sounds of their breathing and their thumping hearts, they were silent. As the heat gradually left their bodies, they gathered themselves up and moved onto other things—talk of how bored they were, how depressed they were, of the boys they'd fooled around with and the boys they hoped to fool around with. This talk was like the hurried motions of pulling on clothes after the spell of intoxication had worn off.

Tess had been thinking about Cath and Kiki a lot since that sixteen-year-old girl went missing.

In the auditorium, Enigma produced a small black drawstring bag filled with black licorice jelly beans and offered it to Tess. She took a single jelly bean and slid it into her jean pocket.

She, Cath, and Kiki used to slip bags of the stuff into their purses before asking a sales clerk at the front of the store to sell them a pack of cigs, which they couldn't very easily steal. Tess stopped eating licorice at the same time she stopped smoking. That was years ago. She was a little afraid to taste licorice now, afraid its pungent taste might make her want something she didn't want to want.

"I'm Tess, Ray's wife," she said, the words sounding dumb and inconsequential.

"Enig," he said.

For lack of something better to talk about, she told him she thought the man in the demonstration pit was a gem.

He said, "The guy speaks softly and uses words like 'companionship,' and you're won over to his side? All your judgments about what these men are doing vanished just like that?"

"What makes you think I had any judgments?"

He stared at her.

"I'm just saying I don't think this guy is like the rest. He's fond of them."

"So what if he is? They're prisoners. They've been yanked up out of their homes. Now they're going to be skinned and fried and made into dashboard ornaments. No pretty talk can justify that."

Then he said, "I'm going to free these poor bastards."

"And do what? Send the snakes out into the arena, the fair tents, the parking lot, the campground, and the carnival?" Even as she said it, she felt a thrill at the idea of the crowds being terrorized by the very animals they came to ogle. There was a lovely justice in it, one that Ray would be unable to appreciate. He disapproved of the event as well, but the difference, she thought, was that Ray's anger arose from a sense of his own suffering at having to bear witness, whereas Enig's anger was for the snakes, for their suffering.

"You heard him—people don't get bitten unless they present themselves as threats." Then, "Lynette tell you what we're going to do with the old man's ashes?"

"Lynette and I aren't close."

"We're going to feed him to the snakes. It's beautiful. That man was a gasser. You know that? He chased them out of their burrows with gasoline. And now he'll disappear into the black holes of the snakes' throats. It's like ouroboros, the snake eating its own tail. It's so damn perfect you can feel it in your gut."

What Tess felt in her gut was something else. She didn't feel bad for Cash. She didn't care what happened to his ashes. They were just carbon and other elements anyhow—elements that would get recycled again and again no matter where they were deposited.

It was Lynette she was thinking about. She'd been married to the man for forty-eight years. How was it that a person could spend her entire adult life with a person she despised so much she'd want to feed his remains to rattlesnakes?

Lynette stepped out of her trailer in a Rockabilly-style black shirt dress like nothing Tess had ever seen her in before. Her long gray hair was pulled back into two French braids.

Enig stepped out of the trailer behind her. He was gargantuan next to Lynette. Together they looked like characters out of a freak show or a fairy tale. He leaned over and kissed her on the mouth, and Tess half expected the kiss to transform Lynette somehow, revealing some hidden identity cast away by a spell.

Ray bristled where he stood with his brothers-in-law Fred and Buck beside Buck's smoker. They drank beer as Buck piled on twenty pounds of pork for the barbeque cook-off because if they were going to come up all this way, might as well take home a trophy.

When Enig broke away from Lynette, he took off walking. He sang as he wove between other people's trailers. He had a voice like caramel—thick and rich and sticky.

Joyce and Trudy hauled the ice chest full of shrimp to a weathered picnic table several dozen yards away, and Lynette and Tess followed with bowls, knives, and newspaper. Ray's sisters didn't know about Lynette's plans for the ashes yet, for if they did, they wouldn't have sat down with their mother to remove the exoskeletons and intestinal tracts from twelve pounds of shrimp, Cash's favorite crustaceans, for dinner.

Joyce said, "I worry about you, Momma."

"What in hell for?" Lynette said.

They had to swat flies with their elbows as they worked, but none of them wanted to smell raw shrimp where they slept, so they battled the flies without complaint.

"The world is one heck of a crazy place right now," Joyce said. She gestured in the direction of the crooning with her eyes.

"You think he's going to bludgeon her in her sleep?" Tess said.

Joyce ignored her. "The two of you don't make any sense."

It was true that Lynette and Enig weren't logical. He was barely one-third her age and had penetrating brown eyes that had probably prompted whole crowds of female fans to offer themselves like trays of skewered fruit. But one thing Tess knew for certain was that lust wasn't logical.

And anyway, Joyce's constant negativity grated her. She was the type of person who would knock senseless fools out of the way to do CPR on you if you were unconscious, but as soon as you were resuscitated, she'd proceed to complain about your halitosis and critique the state of the bra she'd had to pull up around your neck. *How often do you wash that thing? That's not a good color on you, just so you know.*

For this and other faults, Tess wished a meteor would burn through Earth's atmosphere and shoot right through Joyce's skull, a hot little bullet by the time it reached her.

Then she immediately felt guilty for thinking it. There seemed to be an important distinction to be made between recognizing Joyce's despicableness and deriving pleasure from the notion of her suffering for it. The latter had been Cash's territory. If he hadn't been so convinced he could punish people with his actions and words, he would have kept a drawer of voodoo dolls.

"The world has been a crazy place for as long as I've been living in it," Lynette said. She wiped sweat from her forehead with the back of her hand. "Ain't nothing new about crazy."

In no time at all, they were talking about the girl who'd gone missing. The general consensus among Tess's in-laws was that the girl was lying at the bottom of the bayou running through their town, but who did it and how was still up for discussion.

Trudy blew a few strands of her bottle-red hair out of her face and said, "My money's on some shifty-eyed creep like that bagger at Kroger. Every time he asks me if I want help carrying my groceries out, I can see just what he has in mind. He'd scoop me into the trunk of my own car and drive me off to some secret hideout in the woods and do God knows what with me. Then he'd probably dump me and take my groceries and my money to boot."

"Goodness sakes," Joyce said. "What do you think that man could possibly want to do with you?"

"He'd rape her in the rear," Lynette said. "Remember that guy in Alvin who broke into widows' homes and raped them in the rears? Three women in all before he was caught. Same crazy look in his eyes."

Just then, Joyce's second youngest child, Ruth Lily, ran all the way from the carnival to complain that her younger sister, Fern, had bitten her. Ruth Lily held up her arm to reveal human teeth marks. "Take it to your daddy," Joyce said.

None of the women said anything for several minutes. The clouds in the sky were stretched thin like plastic wrap. Tess became painfully aware of how sticky her hands were with the shrimps' inky innards.

"I read that that girl was giving her Momma grief all the time staying out all hours of the night," Joyce said.

Tess slammed the table with her fist, surprising herself as much as her in-laws, who all froze.

People had said terrible things about Kiki when she stole $500 from her grandmother and ran off to Los Angeles. They hadn't known what Tess and Cath had known, that her scurvy stepfather had been molesting her since she was a kid.

They were supposed to have run away together, the three of them, but Kiki had gotten impatient waiting for them to commit. "You're scared," she'd said.

Tess and Cath had been so ashamed of abandoning her that they hadn't even said good-bye. They'd received one letter each from Kiki, in which she'd pardoned them, and then they'd never heard from her again. Their letters to her had come back unopened.

"Let's not blame the victim," Tess said now. She wiped shrimp guts onto newspaper. "Assuming she was abducted, assuming she didn't run away, we all know it was a man who did it."

The other women nodded their heads in agreement.

The talk turned to the violence that lurked beneath the surface of *their* men. Trudy told a story about how Fred punched a man in the stomach simply because he talked to her a little too long about the firmness of cantaloupes as Fred watched from across barrels of apples. "We lit the sheets *that* night," she said with a crooked smile.

Joyce recalled the time Buck repeatedly bashed the earth next to a bush in their back yard with the back of a shovel because she commented that it looked like a rabbit den and the last thing she needed was a whole litter of bunnies getting into her vegetable garden. "He ran out there quick as a snake," she said. "I didn't mean for him to hurt them. I was just saying was all. The whole time I was screaming for him to stop, and after he said he did it for me, so what was I making a fuss about?"

Lynette told a story they all knew—how she'd jumped between Cash and Ray after an eleven-year-old Ray freed the crate of rattlesnakes Cash had caught for the roundup.

Like Enig was scheming to do with the entire arena of rattlesnakes, Tess thought, and she wondered for the first time about Ray's motivation in freeing those snakes. He'd only ever talked about it as an act of kindness, to the snakes, but had it been? Or had it simply been a way to get under his father's skin?

"I thought he was going to kill Ray," Lynette said gravely.

Then she told them something they didn't know, that after that incident, she had no love left for Cash. "If trading him in would have been as easy as returning an expired carton of milk, I would have done it in a heartbeat."

There was a long silence.

Then Lynette said, "I feel like I can tell you this because I know now just what I was missing."

Joyce said, "With all due respect, I don't want to hear about it."

It was supposed to be Tess's turn, but they'd forgotten all about her. No one looked to her. No one said, *So what about Ray? In what ways is he violent?*

Lynette said, "Well, you're going to have to get over it because we're moving in together. We're getting a dog."

"A dog!" Trudy said. "I thought you hated dogs!"

Of course, the story occupying Tess was the one she'd promised Ray she wouldn't tell, and it would humiliate her as much as it would him. She didn't need to give her in-laws another reason to pity them.

"Christ's sake, Momma. Can you slow down for a minute and think about this? He's a kid. Quite frankly, he's a freak too. And you could be that freak's grandmother," Joyce said.

"I've never been happier in my life," Lynette said.

And would it be a stretch to call what Ray had done violent? He was adamant that it had been innocent, that the young woman had misunderstood his intentions. Of course, his actions had indeed conveyed interest. That he wouldn't admit that felt like a kind of violence, the way he'd rather try to convince Tess she was mistaken than own up to the truth. What Tess could never be sure about was whether Ray really was so out of touch with himself that he didn't see this or whether he wanted so badly to believe he had done nothing wrong that he'd convinced himself he hadn't. Or: was he an exceptional liar?

"Momma!" Trudy said.

"Now that's simply a cruel thing to say," Joyce said.

"It's not meant to be cruel. It has nothing to do with you," Lynette said.

Lynette's boyfriend's singing seeped in like a fog. "All you little children, you better lock your doors and clean your mouths." Tess caught a momentary glimpse of his black-clad body in a sliver of empty space between trailers and trees. He was a phantom. He was not of this world. The same could be said of his and Lynette's relationship. Tess would have said that such a love was impossible, impractical, and absurd.

It was as though a fat yellow balloon were being waved in Tess's face. Her in-laws were trying to incite her to strike. They'd been trying all along.

She cleared her throat then and said, "So Lynette, why don't you tell Joyce and Trudy about your plan for their daddy's ashes?"

Lynette cocked her head at Tess. She looked out into the trees where Enig had momentarily passed through.

She said, "Might as well tell you, I guess." She paused. Then, "We're going to feed 'em to the snakes."

All motion stopped at once, but Tess's sister-in-laws' bodies seemed to buzz with the potential for movement like mousetraps that could spring at a feather's touch. Tess wondered if inside an anechoic chamber, she'd be able to hear the twitching of the women's muscles, if together they'd sound like an arena full of rattlesnakes.

Joyce and Trudy stared at Lynette.

"You can't do this, Momma," Joyce said.

"I most certainly can."

Joyce said, "If you want to be rid of them, give the ashes to me. Let me deal with this."

"I want to feed him to the snakes," Lynette said.

"Did that freak put this into your head?" Joyce again.

Trudy looked dazed.

"It's not an idea that really belongs to either one of them," Tess said. "Isn't that right? It blew into you like a divine wind? You listened to your gut and you just knew?" The words were hardly out of her mouth when her hands began to shake just as they had done before her last two appointments with Dr. Olive. She heard the words of the man in the demonstration pit: *They attack out of fear.*

Lynette said, "I lived with that man longer than y'all ever did. Those ashes are mine."

"He's our daddy," Joyce said. "I didn't drive all the way up here for this."

"He gave you both a tough time, too. It wasn't just Ray."

Trudy stood then and took off running toward Lynette's trailer. She let herself inside and came out with the peanut jar.

"Things are going to get ugly if she doesn't hand him back over," Lynette said.

"They're already ugly." Joyce's eyes were on Tess.

As Trudy headed toward the coliseum, Ray grabbed her arm. Tess couldn't hear what was said, but he soon let go and Trudy was off, running clumsily, but faster than Tess would have imagined she was capable of.

"What in hell, Mom?" Ray said as he marched toward the table, but Lynette ignored him. She wiped her hands on the shirt dress and hobbled after Trudy.

Trudy stopped amid the last patch of yellowed grass just before she reached the pavement leading to the fair tents and the food vendors and the crowds of tourists shopping for rattlesnake souvenirs. She twirled around like a sprinkler spraying Cash's ashes in all directions.

When Lynette caught up with her, she got down on her hands and knees and scooped up what she could of the remains while Trudy kicked the ashes around with her feet to save some of her father from her mother.

Tess spit on the newspaper and tried to wipe her hands clean, but they were shaking so bad now that after dropping the paper three times, she gave up.

Joyce yelled to Buck that she was going to clean up, fetch the kids from the carnival, and then they were leaving pronto. She filled the empty plastic bags with the peeled shrimp and piled them back into the ice chest. She wadded up newspaper. She worked fast.

Ray said, "Will someone tell me what the hell is going on around here?"

"Why don't you ask Tess?" Joyce said. She slammed the lid down on the ice chest. She took off for the carnival, which was in the opposite direction of the fair tents and food vendors.

The Ferris wheel, which loomed above the other rides, was motionless except for a slight jiggling, like a cog trying to come unstuck.

Ray turned to Tess. They were on opposite sides of the picnic table, watching each other closely like animals startled in the wild.

Tess stuffed her trembling hands into her pockets and found the jelly bean, sticky now. She imagined a bean stalk so huge it grasped the sky and cast a shadow over the whole damn town of Sweetwater. Would climbing it be an act of bravery or cowardliness? Strength or weakness? This was the sort of questioning that drove Tess crazy. To climb it or not to climb it, the decision could be interpreted so many ways. Like her not accompanying Kiki.

One day not long after that girl went missing, Tess pulled into a random hardware store parking lot, sat in her parked car, and tried to imagine Kiki hitchhiking halfway across the country alone, nothing but a suitcase and a few hundred dollars to her name. How terrified she must have been. Tess's chest ached to think of it.

When she'd considered running away with Kiki, she'd felt as though she were fawning over an unaffordable piece of clothing, like the spangled, gray leather jacket she'd fantasized about for years after she saw it at an upscale boutique she'd had no business browsing. Just do it, one part of her brain had said, while another part calculated interest and all that would have to be sacrificed in exchange.

Practical and cautious, she always placed such preposterous longings back onto their racks and got the hell out of there.

That was one way to look at it.

But what she thought of now was Miss Snake Charmer, the glittery teenage pageant winner who'd donned snake-proof chaps earlier that day and paraded around the inner perimeter of the demonstration pit with a live rattlesnake draped over her outstretched palms like a ceremonial object. Tess recalled the question a reporter called out to the newly crowned Miss Snake Charmer, "Aren't you afraid of all these snakes?" and the girl's answer, "There are a lot scarier things in this world than snakes. Like not fulfilling your dreams. That's the scariest thing I can think of."

PAM'S HEAD

Every time I reach the surface with another load of gel, I pass Pam's head. It's buried beneath loads of the gel, as are her other parts. A calf here, shoulder there. Her parts are visible no matter how much gel we bring up from below because the gel is clear. She's like a mosquito entombed in amber, only more strewn about. We had to tear her apart because she expired below, in the tunnels. Because getting her out of there whole was impossible. I'd never torn a body apart before, never carried another's flesh in my arms. None of us had. But we'd torn apart the gel. We'd lifted and transported the gel. We'd deposited the gel. So we knew what to do. Pam was lifeless, like the gel. And like the gel, she was in the way. So we chiseled apart Pam's body, broke her down into manageable loads. First I carried Pam's left forearm up to the surface. It was a bit unwieldy, but not so unwieldy I needed to chisel it into smaller parts too. Then when I tunneled back down, all that was left was Pam's head. The others had carried out every other piece of her. I didn't even know that I didn't want to touch Pam's head until it was just me and Pam's head, nobody else except Octavia in the distance, far enough away not to be responsible, close enough to see that Pam's head was my responsibility. And so I lifted and transported and deposited Pam's head on the surface near the entrance to one of the oldest tunnels. Because there's work to do. Because building these tunnels is what we do, what we've always done. The tunnels go up to the surface, and they go down. They go horizontal, and they go diagonal. They intersect. Always there is more work to do, more tunnels to be made. Not because we are tunneling toward anything in particular, but because there is gel that hasn't been tunneled. We do not rest. Still, Pam's head. Sometimes when I'm carrying a load of gel up to the surface, I think it's Pam's head that I'm carrying. Then I pass Pam's head, and I look down and see that all I have is gel. There will be other heads, though. Nadia has been slowing for a while now. Sometimes when I tunnel down and she's the only one there, for a moment, I think she has expired. I think I am going to have to tear her apart. But then she starts chiseling again, and so I lift a new load of gel and transport it to the surface again, somewhere along the way forgetting again that it's gel I'm hauling and not Pam's head. And when I see Pam's head again, I pause again and look down again to see what I'm carrying. Maybe this is me slowing too. I guess it's wrong to say we're not tunneling toward anything. We're tunneling toward our deaths, all of us. With each load of gel we transport and deposit, we get closer. Maybe the others look at me now, frozen before Pam's head, and wonder, like I do about Nadia sometimes, whether I've expired. I bet they feel grateful that I'm on the surface. That all they would have to do is deposit around me the loads of gel they're already carrying. They wouldn't have to carry me piece by piece out of the tunnels. They wouldn't have to change course. They wouldn't have to give me much thought at all.

KEY CONCEPTS IN ECOLOGY

Invasive species: A species that is non-native to an ecosystem and that is likely to cause harm to native species.

The creature had been spotted again, and this time, accounts came from two unrelated individuals. The sightings had taken place between the hours of seven and eight that morning, both within a mile of the New Zeniths building. City officials were at that very moment developing a plan of action. What we all needed to do was stay put. This news was delivered by Claudette Bowery, president of New Zeniths, in the lobby at forty minutes after eight. She stood before the plate glass windows that offered a view of the tall pines huddled like football players planning their next play, and she advised us not to leave the building. If we hadn't brought lunch, we should order delivery. Let the deliverers risk *their* lives, Claudette said. That was their job, after all, wasn't it? Not ours. Our work was to furnish world-class instructional content in the subjects of English, math, science, and, increasingly, electives such as woodshop, culinary arts, and cattle-ranch management to the good children across America. And we were just three days out from the date on which Crispin—Claudette's late husband

and the former president of New Zeniths—had promised clients a new interface for administering testlets. My job was to write biology content, but by virtue of being the senior writer in the company, I'd also gotten recruited to test the testlets' interface for functionality. I knew firsthand there was no way we were going to make the deadline. If Claudette knew this, too, she didn't let on. She said, "Now more than ever, we need to pull together and shine. We cannot afford to let anything distract us from that mission."

"Like, say, being torn limb-from-limb by a wild animal," Rhonda Maso, one of the English writers, said to me under her breath.

If we absolutely had to go out to our cars, Claudette said, we should go armed with something we could throw. Not New Zeniths' property, of course, she clarified, but our own possessions, such as water bottles and pill bottles and the knickknacks that littered our desks. "Let me be clear, however, that I have advised you to stay indoors. New Zeniths is not liable for harm that comes to anyone who steps out into the parking lot."

Only once before this had the receptionist, Nan Price, called us unexpectedly via intercom for an emergency meeting in the lobby. That was right after Nine-Eleven. Then, she'd walked around the building passing out little American flags in the same manner that she passed out individual pumps of antibacterial hand sanitizer every October and poison ant traps every April. It was Crispin Bowery who'd delivered the announcement then. We'd all gathered with our flags in hand to listen to Crispin say that in times like these, it was important to stand together. Claudette had held up her little flag and waited for others to do the same, and we had, every last one of us.

This morning's announcement came the day before my forty-fifth birthday. I'd been with New Zeniths seventeen years, twelve years more than I would have predicted on that morning thirteen years earlier when I obediently waved a miniature American flag no larger than an ID card.

Limiting factors: Biotic factors (organisms) and abiotic factors (e.g., soil, light, temperature) that may limit the growth or abundance of an organism or population within an ecosystem.

I used to dream about the day I'd quit my job at New Zeniths, an event that would bring me a banner reading *Good Luck, Andrea*, accompanied by chemical-sludge cookies from the grocery store bakery.

But then Lewis gave up working altogether. He'd always struggled with authority. The man worked a dozen different jobs at least in our first few years together, and in not one case was he fired. He quit, and always with gusto. "That asshole can suck it," he said. Or: "It's lucky I did walk out of there when I did, because if I'd stayed one minute longer, I might have strangled that man. Snapped the ligaments in his neck."

I can't say he pulled a fast one on me exactly. I knew who he was when we got together. I guess I just thought he'd eventually figure out a way to earn an income without feeling like he wasn't being true to himself or whatever. He wasn't a lazy man, and he wasn't without skills. He cooked. He cleaned. He did repairs around the house. I offered him sympathy and sex to keep his confidence up in the ways I knew how.

That thing about snapping neck ligaments, that was in reference to the last boss he ever had, a guy who owned an artisan pizza restaurant. Lewis had assembled and cooked the pizzas in a fancy wood-fired oven. They'd argued about that oven. Lewis thought the guy had been suckered. He thought he could have built him a better oven and for a lot cheaper. The guy told him he wasn't paid to be a consultant; he was paid to make pizzas.

Months ticked by after Lewis quit. Then, years. Lewis stopped looking for work. He expressed no interest in the jobs being advertised around town. Nothing caught his eye, he said. Nothing excited him.

Community: All species within a particular ecosystem, which interact via trophic, competitive, and symbiotic relationships.

My supervisor, Stu Mann, said, "It's always something," before he shut the door to his office. He had a King Kong action figure that swung its arms around and growled when you pressed the button at its feet, and that's what Stu did now.

Tinsel Ware could be heard from the other end of the building yelling at her husband to take off work to pick the kids up from school. "You expect me to trust the schools to keep them safe?!"

Bic Bowery, whose relation to Claudette and Crispin, nobody seemed to know, patrolled the building checking windows and doors for weaknesses a wild animal might take advantage of. When I crossed paths with him in the hallway, he raised his arm up in front of his body like a shield and made a nervous clicking sound.

In the kitchen, Lacy Sears was on the phone with her fiancé. "How does she expect us to focus on work when there's some kind of monster running around out there?" A minute later, she was laughing. "Oh my God, truck driver hats as wedding favors would be so shabby chic! They're ironic. We put our initials on them, *L* and *L*, like we're a trucking company," she said. "Ha! Bananas! Totally!"

Akiko Tanaka, whose hair always had a blunt edge as though she trimmed it every morning, stared out the kitchen window into the bosk behind the building. There in the thicket was a bright red glass toadstool big enough for humans to sit on. Crispin had had it delivered on New Zeniths' tenth anniversary. Beyond the bosk were more pine trees.

There were often animal sightings in the bosk, especially in spring: baby ground squirrels tumbling around the dirt like toddlers, huge heaving lizards, snakes, rabbits, bobcats. Akiko, and others too, passed time watching whatever critter had been spotted. If somebody else entered the kitchen, the spectator would announce the animal and its location. *Armadillo, under that scraggly mesquite.*

Akiko didn't announce anything this morning. She was quiet, her eyes scanning the ground and the trees.

Arnold Dubcheck reached his hand inside the ice machine and came out with a fistful of ice. He said, "I know a guy who saw it. Said it was big as a hippo."

Without turning around, Akiko said, "The largest wild animals in this area are mountain lions."

Arnold shrugged. "A mountain lion as big as a hippo, I guess."

"Adult hippopotamuses weigh about three thousand pounds," I said. "A mountain lion weighs less than the average human adult."

"Whatever," Arnold said.

Akiko smiled at me as she left the kitchen.

If she were a content writer, we might have become friends. As it was, she was a developer, and other than runins in the kitchen, writers and developers didn't fraternize much. We were on opposing teams.

Bic Bowery made a quick beeline for the fridge, grabbed a boiled egg and a pickle, and was out of there without making eye contact with anybody.

"She can't keep us here all night. She can't hold us hostage," Lacy said to her fiancé.

When Noelle Snope and Christie Berry entered the kitchen, they were talking as they often did about what a shitty mom Noelle's sister-in-law was. Noelle had a voice like a reality television star, loud and lilting and self-conscious. "I bet my nephew is running around the back yard unsupervised right this very moment. Snakes, black widows, and now this, whatever the hell this thing is. It's like she thinks her yard is free of all vicious reptiles and insects and monsters."

"Arthropods," I said.

"What?" Noelle said.

"Spiders."

Christie emitted a high-pitched giggle.

That's when Curt Bowery, the elder of the two Bowery sons, entered the kitchen and poured the rest of the drinkable liquid from the coffeepot into his bowl of a mug that read *Curt Bowery, Director of Innovations*. Under that was the corporate logo, a mildly pornographic image of a conical purple mountaintop crowned with a huge gold star. The logo was printed on every test, report, and marketing material. It was on every employee gift—from mugs to paperweights to rape whistles Claudette called "alarm devices." These she'd passed around to the women after a man was stabbed to death at ten o'clock at night at the Shell station down the street. Per the updated policy manual (p. 34), all female employees were advised to have their alarm devices on hand when they exited the building after dark.

"You look at those testlets yet?" Curt said to me.

Everyone else scattered, just like that.

"Since the patch last night?"

Curt smiled, showing too much teeth. "I think we got them this time." He returned the near-empty pot to the hot plate without bothering to switch the machine off.

"The hemipterans?" I said.

Curt stared at me.

"Bugs," I said.

Curt turned toward the window. "I wish the city could say the same for that animal out there." He tossed a paper towel onto the hinged lid of one of the recycling bins, where it stayed put.

"I feel sorry for it."

Curt cocked his head. "That creature shouldn't be roaming around people's workplaces and neighborhoods." Then, "Let me know when you've tested the testlets." He tapped his watch. "Time is running out." He shuffled down the hallway as though he were wearing flip-flops.

Autotrophism: The ability of an organism to synthesize its own food using light energy and inorganic substances.

From time to time, Lewis thought up some idea for generating income, and always he pursued these ideas full throttle, at first. At one point, he was going to make a killing hiring himself out to sort through other people's junk, price it, and sell it. His first and last client was an elderly lady down the street from us. She seemed like a windfall at first. She was living amongst towers of cardboard boxes, like she'd just moved in and hadn't unpacked yet, though she'd been in that house for forty-odd years. When Lewis was done sorting through everything, he discovered she owned eight different hair dryers (eight!). She didn't own anything worth a lot of money, but she owned so much that all of it together could have brought in several thousand dollars easy. Problem one was that, despite having agreed to let him help her sell her stuff, she didn't want to let go of much of anything. I watched Lewis and this little old lady with fingers like fork tines tug back and forth on a rolled-up rug still wrapped in plastic twenty years after she bought it. Problem two was that she fought him tooth and nail over the pricing. Always she wanted more than the damn thing was worth. Those hair dryers, for instance, all of them used, she wanted ten dollars a pop. That you could buy a new hairdryer for the same price held no sway with her.

Another time Lewis got it in his head he was going to make a fortune writing erotica. Never mind that, as far as I knew, he hadn't strung more than a couple of sentences together on paper since he graduated high school, or that Lewis didn't read books period, erotica or otherwise. He set my laptop on a television tray and got to work writing a story about a housewife having sexual encounters with a heating-and-cooling repairman. He did this while he watched football and cooking shows. When I came home in the evenings, he read aloud passages and asked for my input. He was writing from the point of view of the housewife, and in the service of wanting to get it right, he asked questions he'd never asked before. How exactly did I like to have my breasts touched? Did I *really* enjoy the feel of a cock throbbing inside me, or did I just pretend to?

The erotica fell away as quickly as the junk-selling. One day he was calling me at work and reading me sentences that made me blush at my desk, and then another day he'd lost interest. It was the same story with his infused-oils business and his cat-sitting business.

Keystone species: A species that has a disproportionately large effect on its environment relative to its abundance.

I almost collided with Claudette on the way back to my cubicle.

She stood still and stared at me, a wry smile on her lips. She was waiting for something.

"Sorry," I said.

"This is why I'm so meticulous in the policy manual," she said. "Some people think they don't need to be told how to walk through a hallway, but evidence suggests they do."

"My mind was on the testlets," I said.

"I'm sure walking along the right side of hallways instead of the left won't delay the completion of the testlets' interface."

A few months back, when Claudette announced she'd landed a contract with a huge school district we'd been after for years, she'd paused for dramatic effect and, wearing a smile appropriate for a chocolate bar the size of a human head, said, "Let me tell you a secret: I have a magic power."

In Crispin's days as president, we wouldn't have been surprised to hear talk of magic powers. For the State-of-the-Company Address each year, he'd worn a wizard's hat and reiterated the same hyperbole about how New Zeniths was on its way to becoming the top-grossing online curriculum company in the country—this despite the fact that we owned less than half a percent of the market. The day before the Race for the Cure, he'd worn shorts, a T-shirt, and sneakers and jogged through the hallways of the building on the hour, every hour. The point is this: Whereas Crispin had lobbed us like a red clown nose, Claudette struck like a dagger. Even before Crispin's death (bee stings: he was allergic), she'd been the brains behind the business, not to mention the financial manager, the personnel director, the legal consultant, and the chief salesperson all rolled into one.

After another dramatic pause, Claudette had said, "I can stand before a group of people and make them do whatever I want."

I'd known immediately that she'd meant us as much as clients. Just look at all those little Tupperware containers in the refrigerator, all of them the exact same dimensions (p. 28). Claudette sent out an e-mail telling us exercise balls do not make for ergonomic desk chairs, and Deena Gap and Noelle Snope both took theirs home that very day. Claudette made a big to-do about not leaving dishes in the kitchen sink to soak, and poof, people were giving you dirty looks if you let a bowl sit for a few minutes. Claudette inquired one day about the filthy blue pickup truck in the parking lot, wanting to know if it belonged to a vagrant, if she should call the police, and the truck's owner, Christie Berry, showed up to work the next day with the truck so shiny that three birds, apparently blinded by the truck's gleam, flew into Arnold Dubcheck's office window, and Nan had to sweep two of their carcasses (the third mysteriously disappeared) into a dustpan and toss them into the dumpster.

Now, I smiled at Claudette. "Yes," I said, and I continued walking.

Niche: The relational position of a species or population within an ecosystem (e.g., which resources it exploits, its habitat, its place in the food chain).

At my desk, I discovered two e-mails from Nan. The first was a news article link sent to all employees. The portion of text Nan had copied and pasted into the e-mail stated that a team of snipers was being assembled to hunt for the creature. The e-mail reiterated Claudette's warning that we should stay indoors. If we went outside, we not only jeopardized our own safety; we jeopardized the work of the snipers.

The second e-mail was sent to me only, asking which Texas landmark I wanted on my upcoming birthday banner. *Be sure to let me know before lunch, please!*

Birthday banners were four sheets of paper taped together lengthwise, the words *Happy Birthday* _____ bordered by clip art chosen to represent the individual's response to that year's theme—animals the previous year, candy the year before that, hobbies and interests, favorite city, and so forth.

Of forty-seven sub-management employees, only two had just one birthday banner on display in their cubicles, and one of them was Lacy Sears, who had been at New Zeniths for less than a year. Everyone else plastered the banners up and down their cubicle walls like wallpaper. Noelle Snope was the record holder—eighteen years' worth. What she hadn't been able to fit on her walls, she'd taped across the drawers of her filing cabinet.

The only exceptions to this rule were me, Rhonda Maso, and Akiko Tanaka, though, to be honest, I did display the first one for a few months before I looked at it one day and saw it for what it really was. Even now, all these years later, I still feel ashamed that one of those sad scraps of affection once adorned my wall.

Of the six lower-management employees, only one displayed birthday banners, and that was Tinsel Ware, whom everyone believed was promoted for some not-quite-understood political reasons. She came to work in spandex mini-skirts, made only slightly less scandalous by the loose, shapeless tops she wore with them. Every e-mail she produced was so grammatically strange it sometimes took ten minutes to puzzle out one sentence. She interrupted people midstream and took her shoes off at meetings, sometimes picking polish, always blue and always sparkly, off her toenails while she spoke.

The office walls of upper management were bare except for framed degrees.

Carrying capacity: The maximum population size of a species that an environment can sustain given the available resources (see Limiting Factors).

One morning a few months back, Lewis said, out of the blue, that he had good news. I'd learned by then to be skeptical. I said nothing. I waited.

"I didn't want to say anything too soon, in case I was terrible at it. I couldn't take another disappointment, but, well," and he paused and smiled, then said, "I've been taking acting classes! I'm pretty good at it, Andrea. I mean, like, really good. That's what the teacher says. And don't worry—I worked out a bartering system with her. I'm doing repairs on the acting studio. It's kind of run down, plenty of work to keep me paid up for months. It's not costing us a dime. I've been going for several months now, and, shit, this is the best thing that's ever happened to me!"

We were seated in our little kitchen at the ugly yellow dining table I'd wanted to replace for years, and I startled as the cuckoo bird thrust out of its wooden pentagon box, which was long on the bottom half and squat on top, like a vampire coffin.

I said, "Acting. Huh."

He said, "The teacher says I have a natural talent. There could be money in acting. I mean, there is money in acting. People make shitloads of money acting. Why not me? If no one ever believed in themselves enough to take a risk, think how much we wouldn't have. Airplanes, rocket ships, you name it."

I stared at him.

Lewis said, "I was worried you might react this way, but then I thought, no, Andrea loves me. She'll be happy for me."

I knew well that the stress of being jobless can make people desperate and irrational. Sometimes people in Lewis's situation pick up an addiction. They start drinking heavily, and when their partner tries to help them kick the habit, they hide the alcohol in whacked places, like emptied bleach jugs. I'd been on the lookout for that type of thing. I had not been prepared for this.

And now here I was, seated inside my little cubicle, tasked with selecting a Texas landmark for my birthday banner, while Lewis was probably, at that very minute, pretending to be someone other than himself. If I could have traded places with him, I would have done it in a heartbeat.

When I was younger, I never imagined working a forty-hour-a-week office job, in a cubicle no less. When Lewis and I moved in together, I'd believed I would work just long enough to fatten up our savings account so I could quit and start up a photography business. I'd thought I would be a nature photographer, sell my work at art fairs and cafés and on commission. Our savings account never really fattened, though. I can't tell you where the money went. We didn't budget in those early years, this was true, but it's not like we traveled Europe or bought fancy cars either. When I try to think where it went, all that comes to mind is mundane, routine shit like car tires and air conditioners.

That's what I was thinking about when I fired off my response to Nan. *Waco*, I typed.

Almost immediately, she came back with *What landmark is in Waco?*

The Branch Davidians' compound or, heck, a picture of David Koresh himself.

Competition: A negative interaction between organisms (or populations or species) in which both require the same limited resource(s).

"Close the door, please," Stu said. Then, "David Koresh?!" He laughed. Then he immediately grew serious. "How is David Koresh a Texas landmark?"

"At the very least, Waco is a landmark because of him. That was my original request. I just included his name to clarify when Nan asked what landmark was in Waco."

"You and I both know Waco isn't on anybody's list of Texas landmarks."

"Whose list? Was there a list I was supposed to choose from? Because I never received that list," I said.

Stu sighed.

"Me too, Stu. Me too."

"Do you really want a banner with a picture of David Koresh on it?" he asked.

"If I have to have a banner, then yes."

"Why didn't you just say you didn't want a banner?"

"Is that an option? It wasn't presented as an option."

"OK look, I know you've had it testing the interface for testlets. I know it's a waste of your time, and I'm sorry about that, but if we don't do it, we have to listen to Curt and his people go on about how the reason we don't have testlets is because the content writers don't want to write content. We have to keep showing that it's not us; it's them."

"I bet you a million dollars that seventy-five percent of the bugs I reported yesterday are still there," I said.

"I know. I know. But, see, Nan is the real victim here. She knows that if she puts up a banner with a picture of David Koresh, she's going to hear from Claudette, and so now she's forced to take this request to Claudette to find out what she should do, make the banner or don't make the banner. Then Claudette comes to me, and now I'm talking to you. And that's a waste of a lot of people's time, too."

"Nan goes on about how she loathes Claudette, but she loves, loves, loves to take shit to Claudette. I've seen her with her notepad and pencil, recording when people leave ten minutes early. I've seen her in the kitchen jotting down the names of who took up more than their share of refrigerator space."

Stu stared at me. "So you don't want a banner? Do I have that right?"

"I do not."

"I'll tell Claudette. Thank you."

Predation: A trophic interaction in which individuals of one species (the predator) kill and consume individuals of another species (the prey).

Starting at noon, the building was visited by a wave of delivery guys toting sandwiches, pizzas, tacos, you name it. Nan sat behind the reception desk and dialed extensions, and when individuals didn't answer, she called them to the lobby via intercom. "Arnold, please come to the lobby to pick up your food." "Stu, please come to the lobby to pick up your food."

The delivery guys brought more than food. The one who delivered Rhonda Maso's gluten-free Greek pizza said he'd just finished delivering pizzas to the police station, and he'd seen half a dozen men in full camouflage. They were talking strategy, how they planned to take the creature by tranquilizer if they could, but they'd be prepared to shoot to kill if they had to. The guy who delivered my chicken burrito said he'd seen a flash of something huge and furry in the pines just across the street as he was on his way to New Zeniths. The town was so quiet that he'd been startled by the slam of a car door earlier, hence the salsa stain on his pants.

At about the time that everyone but Nan, who fasted two days a week, had finished their food, that's when we heard the first round of gunfire.

I counted six shots, but some of my coworkers claimed to have heard more. Tinsel Ware said, "I have super good hearing. Perfect pitch, too. There were twelve shots." She leaned over and rested her breasts against the kitchen counter as she ground coffee beans. Arnold Dubcheck stood there and argued that there'd been eight shots, but when Tinsel stood upright again, he walked away.

Barely a cup's worth of coffee had brewed when Curt Bowery entered the kitchen and filled his cup, oblivious to Tinsel standing by the pot, waiting.

"Did you test the testlets yet?" he said to me.

"Five times in the last two weeks," I said.

"I sent you an e-mail nearly an hour ago. I really need you to test them pronto. See if we took care of the big bugs, the deal breakers." His neck, or what little part of it was visible over the top of his navy blue turtleneck, was beet red.

"What makes something a deal breaker or not a deal breaker? As far as I'm concerned, everything I've reported is significant. Every last bug."

He laughed nervously. "How about you just report whatever you find?"

"What about Bic? Isn't this his job? I guess I just don't understand what Bic's job is exactly. I thought he was paid to do quality control."

"You're paid to do it, too." Curt smiled and stood a little straighter. "Your job description says ... *and other responsibilities that come up*. All our job descriptions here at New Zeniths include that phrase. That flexibility is part of what allows us to accomplish as much as we do with a staff of about sixty." He'd taken the words straight out of his mother's mouth.

I said nothing.

"Ball's in your court," Curt said as he walked away.

Akiko Tanaka entered the kitchen and looked out the window again. I joined her. She turned and gave me a solemn smile. "I hope they missed," she said. "I hope that animal is fast."

"Me, too," I said. "Me, too."

Parasitism: A symbiotic relationship between species in which one species (the parasite) benefits, while the other species (the host) is harmed.

When I returned to my desk, there was an e-mail from Claudette: *I feel it is my duty to remind you at this time that you can sign on for disability insurance at any time you wish. Of course, you are not required to enroll, and New Zeniths does not pay for disability insurance premiums, but please remember that New Zeniths does not pay for time off due to disability or extended illness.*

The first thing I thought was that she envisioned me being mauled by that animal out there. When I realized that what she was really alluding to was my birthday, that forty-five signaled my decrepitude somehow even though Claudette was twenty years my senior, I did what I often did at moments like these at work: I closed my eyes and breathed. When I opened my eyes again, I tested the testlets. If I dared put it off any longer, Curt or Claudette would say I was responsible. Why don't we have testlets? Because Andrea had better things to do than QC.

Just as I was about to send another email full of bugs to Curt, I turned to find him staring intently at my computer screen. I startled. He smiled as though he'd intended for this to happen.

"So?" he said. He appeared to be trying to read what I'd written.

"I was just about to send it to you," I said.

"Why don't you just tell me what you found?"

"It's kind of a lot to sum up. How about you read what I've documented and then let me know if you have questions?" I said.

The blush crept up Curt's neck again. He took a deep breath. "Look, nobody expects the interface to be perfect at this point. All we need is basic functionality. The bells and whistles come later."

"It's not my call what's basic and what's a whistle. Isn't that your job? Or should I copy Claudette on this?" I said.

Curt closed his eyes for a moment. "That won't be necessary," he said when he opened them. "Just send it to me, please." He started to walk away, but then turned back toward me. He pointed to his watch. "It's nearly two in the afternoon. Almost an entire day lost."

"Just trying to do a thorough job," I said. I pressed the send button.

A little while later, Stu called me into his office again. He leaned back in his chair, which was black leather to my magenta canvas, and said, "Now I have Claudette asking me why it took you so long to test the interface."

"Good old Curt doing what he does best," I said.

Stu looked tired. "What do you want me to do? You want me to tell Claudette you think her son isn't pulling his load?"

Weight, I corrected in my head. Weight, not load. "No, I don't think that would be a good idea."

The way Stu stared at me, it was as though I were back in the third grade, being accused by my teacher, Mrs. Pell, of tattling on another kid in class, a boy I'd seen scratching the F-word into the seesaw's red paint with the key he wore around his neck on fuzzy yarn.

"It's just that this stuff isn't good for employee morale," I said. "Already there's almost no recognition of who around here works hard and produces quality work. No distinction is made. Last year it was made public that everyone in the company got the same percent raise no matter the differences in our performances. That kind of thing doesn't inspire people to work hard. It doesn't inspire greatness."

"Greatness?!" Stu laughed.

I was thinking not just of Curt, but of Arnold Dubcheck, who could be heard snoring every morning between approximately the hours of 10 and 11:30, sometimes in the afternoons too; and Lacy Sears, who was almost always either talking on the telephone or texting; and Noelle Snope and Christie Berry, who spent two hours a day, easy, gossiping in one of their cubicles or, more often than not, the middle of the hallway. That was just my side of the building. Hector Mendez played video games half the day, and he wasn't even sly about it. Tinsel Ware changed into a leotard and tights every day at noon and proceeded to do yoga and Pilates in her office until well past the end of her lunch hour.

It occurred to me now that perhaps my coworkers, whom I'd despised all this time for their laziness and mediocrity, were actually smarter than me. What had my work ethic gotten me? I'd been with New Zeniths for seventeen years. I made a decent salary, that much was true, but I had yet to graduate to an office. I got absolutely not one atom of respect from management. And I was pretty certain I wasn't paid any more, or not much more, than my much less productive coworkers.

What would it take for me to finally accept that I was busting my ass for myself, and no one and nothing else? What did this make me but the biggest fool in the company?

As I stood to leave Stu's office, another round of shots was fired. This time I counted nine.

Soon after that, Claudette announced via e-mail that water was pooling behind the building. There was a leak in the plumbing. A sniper bullet, she mused. A plumber was on his way, and the water would be shut off for much of the afternoon. If we were thirsty, Nan kept bottled water at reception for homeless people who occasionally wandered in off the street asking for a drink. If we needed to use the restroom, the toilets could be used, though they could not be flushed; or we could leave the building, but we were strongly advised to use supreme caution, traveling in groups of three or four preferably. If we did choose to leave to use a restroom elsewhere, she noted, no PTO would be deducted from our accounts.

Biogeochemical cycles: Pathways by which chemical substances (e.g., carbon, nitrogen, water) move through both biotic and abiotic components of Earth.

Two men worked out back shoveling dirt and mud to expose the building's plumbing. Neither seemed the least bit concerned about being outdoors while snipers were, at that very moment, hunting a wild animal.

Arnold Dubcheck didn't seem the least bit concerned about the toilets not flushing. He was in the bathroom for four or five minutes, and then, as usual, he stuck his bare hand into the ice bin.

Lacy Sears, earbuds in her ears, pink phone in hand, said, "God, Lawson, it's like she thinks we're animals."

If she hadn't been on the phone, I might have informed her that we, in fact, are animals, but I resisted. Anyway, she had a point. Had Claudette really meant to suggest we may wish to opt to use the non-flushing toilets? Did she really think that little of us?

On some level, I didn't blame her. Just look at all those birthday banners. Claudette had to have noticed them. The woman was sharp, the way she stared at you across the conference table with those dead shark eyes. She probably thought every last one of those people was an idiot.

But if Claudette thought any differently of Rhonda, Akiko, and me, I sure as hell couldn't tell. We didn't have offices like Tinsel Ware did.

Just as I was getting desperate for a bathroom myself, Nan announced via intercom that the water was back on temporarily, for about ten minutes, should we wish to use the restrooms at this time.

When I entered the restroom, I found that the toilet in

the open stall was clogged with shit and toilet paper. The shoes on the floor in the other stall belonged to Claudette. On any other day, I would have left the restroom and come back, but given the limited window of time, I waited. As usual, Claudette flushed before she pulled out a toilet seat cover and sat down. Why she did this, what it was about, was a thing I was curious about. Did she think she was protecting herself from flecks of someone else's feces flinging up out of the water like microscopic Godzillas? After flushing a second time, she came out of the stall, and she said, "How's your husband's job search going?"

Lewis had been out of work for nearly ten years at that point, and still this was the only thing Claudette ever bothered to ask me about.

"Nothing yet," I said.

"It's a tough economy," Claudette said.

"Yes," I said, though it pained me to agree with her, as though I were admitting I was trapped smack dab where I was.

It was only when she turned toward the sink that I noticed the tissue seat cover tucked into the seat of her pants like a lobster bib. I stood there frozen in place.

Claudette raised her eyebrows. "Were you going to say something?" her reflection said to me.

"I," I said. I stopped.

Claudette turned toward me. She grabbed a paper towel from the dispenser on the wall next to me. She was still watching me, waiting. She looked impatient. "Well?"

If I told her, she would resent me for it. If I didn't tell her, she'd parade around the office with that seat cover flapping after her like a flag. Her humiliation would be tenfold. While the thought of this was pleasant, to be sure, she would eventually conclude that I'd chosen not to spare her this.

She shook her head and started to turn toward the bathroom door. That's when I blurted out, "Wait! You have a toilet seat cover hanging from the back of your pants." I said it quickly before she could meet my eyes.

"What?" Claudette said, as though she hadn't understood. She reached down and felt the thing, and the brief moment of panic that overcame her face was precious. She muttered about not knowing how it had gotten there, as though it had jumped from the wall and attached itself to her like a squid. She returned to the stall to remove it, and I had to wait again for my turn to use the restroom. Claudette flushed the seat cover and rushed out of the restroom without uttering a word of gratitude.

My relief over finally getting to use the toilet was short-lived, for when I went to flush, nothing happened. I tried again and again, but no matter what direction I moved the handle or how long I held it, my turd just floated there. It seemed impossibly long, like it couldn't have fit in my intestines. I thought then about all the shit generated every day by the employees of New Zeniths. And what about over the course of a week, a month, a year? I knew about sewers and waste-treatment plants, but still, I couldn't fathom it. Cities full of shit funneling into these plants day after day after day.

I heard Lewis's words: "Life is serious shit, Andrea. If there's something you want to do, you need to do it. You need to go after it. You don't get another chance. This is it!" He'd waved his arms as though he were conducting an orchestra. "I've realized that now. I've been forced to think hard about what I really want, what I really care about."

"Find a way to make it pay the bills, and I don't care what you do," I'd said.

"I'm not an idiot for thinking it's possible to make money acting. It is possible. You've got to be optimistic about things, or otherwise, what's the point?"

"And human-engineered sea vessels explore ocean trenches, but that doesn't mean I can build one."

"Maybe that's your problem. You've said it yourself. You lack confidence."

"I don't have the luxury to do what I want, Lewis," I'd said.

Of course, that wasn't really true. I could walk out and never come back, and nobody could stop me. People quit jobs every day, regardless of whether they can afford to or have other job prospects. I simply wasn't that sort of person. I was the type of person who stammered in front of her boss, wasting the last few minutes of flush time. I was the type of person who felt smug about rebelling against birthday banners, while the rest of my co-workers put their feet up all day. I was the type of person who picked up their slack.

As I left the bathroom, I passed Rhonda Maso on my way to the kitchen.

"If that animal's smart, it should be halfway across the state by now," she said, shaking her head.

"I hear that," I said.

I entered the kitchen, which was empty, and I headed straight out the back door and into the bosk. I sat on Crispin's toadstool and faced the pines. Around me, bees buzzed, lizards scurried up and down tree trunks, mourning doves cooed. No sign of anything out of the ordinary. Then I turned back towards the building and saw Akiko Tanaka staring out the kitchen window at me.

VENTRILOQUY

In all their seventy-five years, the girls had never seen anything like the hospital surplus sale. The lobby was full of shining, silvery treasures. It was like a Christmas dream come true. Cadaver carts on wheels sparkled like winking knives. Slender IV drip poles were poised along the wall across from the information desk, so that to Georgine, they looked like ladies waiting for dances. Maureen thought they looked like cats ready to pounce.

"Aren't they the daintiest things?" said Georgine.

"And ferocious," said Maureen.

But the item that stole their attention was a real oddity. It was hardly the kind of thing they would have expected to find at the sale. It was the kind of thing you don't know you're looking for until one day, there it is, and immediately you know you have to have it.

It was a little man just under three feet tall. He had the roundest head they had ever seen, and bright, ruddy cheeks. His scalp was smooth and hairless. It shone like the surrounding silver. He wore brown leather shoes that must have been made for a child, and his little button-up shirt was thin and fragile, like ancient paper. The red bowtie around his neck was thick, and they thought that if they pulled it, they might find the bowtie attached to his throat by string and that he might speak as the string inched its way back inside him, returning the bowtie back to its place.

They each felt a surge of blood through their veins so swift that they grabbed hold of one another's arms to steady themselves. They felt woozy.

Georgine thought of the smell of pencil lead that has set in a drawer for ninety-nine years. Maureen thought of a glass marble encased in a bottle cap eye socket, buried beneath six inches of dirt at the edge of a porch, its location marked by a ceramic duck.

"Oh," said Georgine.

"Oh," said Maureen.

"A daddy doll," they said together.

The way the little man seemed both dead and alive excited them. They wanted this little man more than anything they had ever wanted in their entire lives, and this wanting made their stomachs weak. They piled cadaver carts and IV poles into their trunk, and they set the little man between them on the front seat.

They were silent for a while, the feel of his old-man thin shirt against their arms setting their hearts aflutter. Georgine imagined doing his laundry, ironing his tiny boxer shorts. She imagined giving him a bath in the kitchen sink, as if he were a dog or a baby. Maureen imagined flossing his teeth for him and spanking him for not putting the toilet seat back down.

"We'll go to the park," said Georgine.

"The one with the pond," said Maureen.

When they got there, and the little man didn't move, Georgine carried him against her shoulder. She patted his back as if she were burping him.

"By the bridge?" asked Georgine.

"Indeed," said Maureen.

Georgine set him down by a wooden footbridge crossing a little pond with cattails and geese. Maureen broke off a third of her pork and pepper sandwich and placed it next to the little man's legs.

"It is always pretty here," said Georgine.

"It rains just when you least expect it," said Maureen.

The little man sat stock still. He did not seem to notice the sandwich. This surprised them because the aroma of the pork and peppers was difficult to resist. Surely, if the little doll man could breathe—for his little chest expanded with tiny breaths—he could lift his hand to get a taste of the sandwich. What kind of a doll man breathed but didn't eat?

"You could take your shoes off and dangle your feet in the water," said Georgine to the little man.

"Or you could go swimming," said Maureen. "We have towels in the trunk."

Nothing from the little man.

Georgine thought he was probably just sad. He must miss the hospital. Perhaps he had a family. Maureen thought he might be deaf or mute. She considered yelling directly into his ear.

"Maybe we should take him back," whispered Georgine.

"Maybe," whispered Maureen. She moved closer to the little man. Like a doctor, she examined his eyes and ears. She pulled lightly at the bowtie on his neck. He was still. He did not look at her.

Georgine patted the little man's smooth scalp. She lifted his arms and let them fall. She picked up his feet and moved them to see that his knees worked.

Maureen felt to see whether he had ribs and how many. She laid her fingers in the tiny grooves of them. She imagined lacing her fingers through, the way people clasp hands, fingers intertwined, when times are bad.

"This is the church, and this is the steeple," said Maureen.

"But where are all the people?" said Georgine.

Maureen placed her fingers on his lips, which seemed too warm. She then pushed her forefinger into his mouth, which had no teeth to guard it. When she'd pried his mouth open, using both her hands, the girls pressed their cheeks together and peered in.

What they saw astounded them. His uvula blinked and stared like a drooping eye. And in it they saw their own faces, but not as they had been that morning when they'd checked the mirror on their way out of the house. These were the faces of adolescents, almost unrecognizable after so many years. Their cheeks looked chubby and smooth in comparison to what they had seen in the mirror earlier that day. Their eyes were like chocolate buttons, wide and so present, not yet settled back into their skulls.

They had not looked into these faces in years, not even in photographs. The only childhood photographs either of them owned lay in the bottom of a chest of old records and hats with feathers and folds. Since their record player had long ago quit, and they had new hats with balls and stems on top, there had been no need to open the chest. What they saw reflected in the uvula were remembrances of a time they did not like to think about. These faces, heavy with memories, pained them. They felt the prick of the spindle needle sixty-five years after.

"At least we look good," whispered Georgine.

"But we're little girls," said Maureen, with some panic.

"I don't remember having such golden curls. I'd thought they were straw."

"It's a spell. We mustn't look."

"Oh," said Georgine. "What should we do?"

"We'll leave him here," said Maureen. "There's water, and he can find other things to eat if he doesn't like what we've given him. There are nuts and leaves."

Maureen closed the little man's lips. Then she said loudly, "Do you hear that? We're going to leave you here if you don't speak up. You're going to have to fend for yourself."

"Perhaps he's in a coma. Perhaps he's been in a coma for so long that the hospital gave up on him," Georgine said.

"Or he's nothing but a puppet," said Maureen. "A dummy whose master passed away."

"We'll forget about him," said Georgine.

"And everything will be like it was," said Maureen

They were halfway to standing when they thought they heard a sound, a faint whistling like a motor. It seemed to be coming from the little man's belly. They looked away. It was nothing, they thought. It was in their heads, and it would stop at any moment. They waited.

Then Georgine spoke. "Maybe he's a wind-up."

"That's harmless enough," said Maureen.

"Yes. He must have a motor in his tummy."

"If he has a motor, then we can turn him off."

"I'll look for a switch. Maybe in the small of his back."

They hunched down again, and they lifted his torso and felt for a switch. They found nothing.

"The sound doesn't seem to be slowing. Shouldn't it be slowing?" said Georgine.

"What if instead of a motor it's a bomb?" said Maureen.

"Well," said Georgine. "If it's a bomb, we have to get rid of it."

They laid their ears against his chest. They strained to listen, and then they heard something in his chest turning like cogs in a music box. It seemed he was playing a song for them.

Georgine heard a tune her father had sung to her. When he'd sung the song he'd tapped the rhythm out on her nose. Mostly, the rhythm had been bouncy and soft, but there was a part in which the taps got harder and more insistent. When she'd been just a baby there was barely a difference between those taps and the others, but as she grew older, her father tapped a little harder and harder still. Though her father never hurt her, something about those harder taps used to embarrass and anger Georgine. Then one time, to even out the score, she echoed the song on her father's nose. When it came time for that particular part, she tapped his nose harder than he'd ever tapped hers. She tapped his nose with enough force that she thought she might bruise him. He had looked surprised, and she thought he had winced, but he covered it up with a chuckle. *Why you sure are fierce*, he'd said, and he never played the song on her nose again.

Maureen heard a song she recognized from the carnival she'd lived a few blocks from as a child. Her father had given her a few bills almost every Saturday evening and told her to go to the carnival and stay there until he came to take her home. He would send her out just before the sun went down, and often he did not come for her until close to midnight. He gave her enough money for dinner, which was usually a hotdog, a soda, and cotton candy; the rest she spent on rides. Maureen's favorite ride at the carnival had been the one that spun her around and around, so quickly that she felt her skin might slip off her skeleton, and that she would leave the ride not as one girl, but two—one skin, one bone.

Georgine and Maureen both pulled their heads away

from his chest. They took in deep breaths, and they exchanged looks of panic.

"We have to do something," they said.

"We can't leave him here. Little children and animals might play with him," said Georgine.

"He might blow them to bits," said Maureen.

"Exactly," said Georgine.

"We must send him afloat in the pond. It's the safest thing."

"Like a lily pad."

"Like Ophelia."

Together they lifted the little man. Georgine took his head and shoulders and Maureen his legs and feet. They carried him a few yards and set him on the water. They gave him a push. The water soaked his clothes and began to swallow all but his head, which floated on the surface like a hollowed-out melon.

"Bye-bye," they said.

"You stay out there now," said Georgine.

"Don't ever come back," said Maureen.

WHEN THE COTTONMOUTHS
COME TO FEED

The morning a young man opened fire on students and faculty at the university my older daughter, Katya, attended, I watched two cottonmouths glide across the koi pond as gently as paper boats.

The evening before I'd sat by the pond with my five-year-old daughter, Raya: no snakes. I'd gazed down at the pond from my bedroom window when I awoke: no snakes. That put their arrival at somewhere between approximately six and seven that morning. Katya was killed between 6:33 and 6:41. For eight minutes the man had fired his gun before police "took him out" as a radio reporter put it, as though talking about a sports match. Eight minutes is nothing if you are reading or decorating a cake, but if you're killing people, eight minutes is a long time.

That morning by the koi pond, I didn't know yet about Katya. All I knew was that two cottonmouths were circling above the eleven koi—Petra's koi. My wife had dug the pond herself, six years ago. Four was the number of years I'd been without her.

The koi swam back and forth in figure eights as though the cottonmouths were mere sticks adrift above them. Or maybe they simply knew there was nowhere to escape to, nowhere to hide. In any case, their ease put me at ease. Or let's just say I was at ease. I can't really say why.

Less than an hour after three bullets emptied Katya's blood through her back and chest, the sun rose between the spread branches of the pecan tree at the far edge of my yard. The horsetail reeds rattled in the breeze. The black snakes cornered two koi against the shallowest bank of the pond and unhinged their jaws to expose their namesake white throats. They caught the koi by their heads. The fish wriggled like ballerinas on their toes.

At nearly two feet long and twenty pounds apiece, the koi seemed too big for the cottonmouths to swallow. Yet when I returned after dropping Raya off at school and before I headed to the bakery, there were only nine koi in the pond. The cottonmouths had vanished.

It wasn't until the fourth photograph that I saw Katya. I recognized the light blue dress and neon orange sneakers, the ugliest sneakers in the world, I'd once said to her. The color of a life vest, I thought, as if my brain was trying to plant jokes where jokes wouldn't grow. Still, the sneakers' garishness was lucky insofar as I identified Katya without having to endure a closer look.

I'd bought that dress for her when she visited at Christmas. By bought I mean I gave my credit card information to an online retailer after Katya said it was what she wanted in lieu of the bicycle I'd gifted her. "I can't very well haul a bicycle overseas." As far as I knew, she hadn't pinned down a particular destination but she was determined to go somewhere far away after graduation this spring. Now I had no reason to concern myself with such details.

What I did have to concern myself with was the cat she'd left behind in the apartment she'd shared with two other girls. The father of one of the girls called to settle the matter of the cat, Prince Boo.

"Katya never told me about a cat," I said.

We agreed that the girls wouldn't be there when I picked up Katya's belongings, that they'd leave the key under the mat. They couldn't handle it, the father said. I laughed, then stopped.

When I entered the apartment, I found six cardboard boxes stacked on the living room floor. One had a hole cut into the top, from which poked the head of a duck, carved from wood. The handle of an umbrella. Prince Boo sat on the windowsill. He turned toward me, then back to the window.

I peeked into the bedrooms. The doors weren't closed. The third room was vacated, the mattress bare. I tried to imagine what it had looked like when Katya was living in it. When Katya was still living. I hadn't visited the university since I dropped her off three years ago, freshman year.

The boy who'd killed her and her peers was twenty-three years old. He'd had a room somewhere, too, though probably the parents weren't allowed to touch anything, not even to look.

I imagined they were grateful for this.

"You got us a cat!" Raya said when Vicky brought her back. If it weren't for the cottonmouths, I might have asked Vicky to stay over at my house to watch Raya, but Vicky didn't have children of her own, and I had visions of Raya lying dead on the ground a good half-hour before Vicky realized she was missing. Raya was all I had left.

"It was Katya's," I said. "Its name is Prince Boo. Katya named it Prince Boo."

Vicky gave me a crazy look, but not too crazy. We'd been dating for only four months and weren't at a point where she would expect me to run pet adoptions by her.

"Prince Boo," Raya said. "Come here and let me eat you." She put her forehead to the cat's belly and rubbed it around.

Vicky removed containers of barley soup, meatballs, and marinara sauce from a blue cloth grocery bag. "Not as good as anything you make, but I figured you wouldn't be picky."

My mother had introduced me to Vicky. In fact, Vicky was the third woman she'd introduced me to since Petra died. To these women, I'd apologized, said I had nothing to give. The first two smiled uncomfortably, said they understood. Not Vicky. She'd said, "You don't have to give me anything." Then she leaned forward and kissed me, on the mouth, right there in the restaurant. I kissed her back. I grabbed her shoulders and felt like I might never let go. When she pulled away, she blushed and confessed to having had a couple of glasses of wine before I picked her up.

Now, she put her arms around me and pressed her ear against my chest as if checking my vitals. "So, how did it go?"

"She died wearing those hideous orange shoes. You need an umbrella?"

Vicky pulled away.

"I need an umbrella!" Raya said. "Mine's broken. Remember?"

"This is an awful lot for one person to take on," Vicky said. The way she looked at me, I wasn't sure if she meant me or her.

"Two more fish are missing. We're down to seven," I said.

"Why don't you call that snake guy?" Vicky said.

"I will. I'm just tired."

"Oh, Lev! Of course, you are. I'll take care of it for you."

"That's not what I mean. I'll do it."

She shrugged. "Should I stay over?"

I told her I was wiped out and would probably go to bed at the same time as Raya, but what I did was stay up and research cottonmouths. I learned that they're solitary. The only time they're seen together is when mating or when a mother has just given birth to young.

A few days later, I spotted the snakes through the window while I brushed my teeth in the morning. When I reminded Raya not to let Prince Boo out of the house, she begged to go see them. We walked out there slowly. I'd read that the aggressive behavior cottonmouths were known for was a myth, but I didn't want to take any chances. Also, I didn't want to scare them away.

Raya brought along her doll, Ms. Stein, which had gray hair and a scrunched up face like an old lady, and set it next to her on the mosaic bench. Petra had made the mosaic when she was pregnant with Raya. Katya had been fifteen. We hadn't intended to have a second child. When you have just one child, you can give her the entire pastila in its perfect, unbroken form. When you have two, you have to split the pastila into two crumbly, asymmetrical halves, or so that's how a second child had seemed to me in the abstract, before I'd held Raya in my arms.

Katya left for college soon after Petra died, so it had been just me and Raya ever since. Raya was too young to remember Petra, and Katya's distance in age and geographic location made her seem more like an aunt than a sister. Thus, according to Raya, the three koi on the mosaic bench represented me, her, and her doll, Ms. Stein.

The snakes were each about three and a half feet long. If they were mating, then it was a strange, prolonged courtship, consisting of gorging themselves on fish for over a week.

"Could they eat a cat?"

"They've eaten four koi, so yeah, I think it's safe to say they could eat a cat."

Raya considered this. "Or Prince Boo could scratch their heads off."

"I don't think so. I mean it about Prince Boo. That cat's as good as dead if you let it out here."

"They look like ice skaters," Raya said.

"Did you hear me about the cat?"

The snakes cornered two more koi. There was a flash of white before they latched on just as they'd done that first morning. The koi's bodies wriggled, and the snakes' heads rocked back and forth with them. Raya gripped my knee. I put my hand on hers. We didn't say a word.

This, I suppose, was when I started thinking that the snakes were Petra and Katya, though later I felt as though I'd known it all along. Sitting there with Raya, watching the snakes fill their mouths with the fish I'd fed for four years, I was pleased. As if I'd cooked a meal and was watching the people I love enjoy it, only the people in this case were a pair of ravenous pit vipers.

Raya said, "How could they eat those fish when the fish are so fat?"

"The snakes are flexible," I said, though I wasn't satisfied with my own answer.

"How can they be so hungry?"

After Petra died, Katya hardly touched food. An apple and a slice of cheese, and she'd say she felt stuffed. Sometimes pain is a bottomless pit that needs to be filled,

like hunger; sometimes it is the need to preserve that bot-
tomlessness. Or deepen it.

When I took Raya to school, she told her teacher, Agnes, about
the snakes. "I saw the food chain in our pond this morning."

Agnes's eyes got big. "Did you?"

It wasn't snakes Agnes wanted to talk to me about. "I'm
tremendously sorry for your loss. You should have told me
about Raya's sister. I need to know if the behavior I see in
class might be related to something going on outside of
the classroom."

"Is there some behavior I should know about?"

"That's what concerns me. It's like nothing's happened at all."

"She saw Katya only a few weeks a year. They're seventeen
years apart in age."

Raya's memories of Katya were almost as limited as her
memories of her mother. At best, trips to the beach, Katya
taking her to see Cirque dus Soleil.

Also, Raya wasn't uncomfortable with the topic of death
the way some children are, the way many adults are. The day
I introduced Raya and Vicky to each other, along the way
to dinner, we got stuck at a light behind a long line of cars
waiting to turn left. "This light's so slow," Raya said, "we'll
probably be dead by the time it turns green."

Vicky got a funny look on her face. "I'm pretty sure that's
not going to happen."

"Everybody dies," Raya had said.

Agnes gave me a sympathetic look. "Well, we'll have
you in to make kulich with the kids another time. When
you're ready."

"What? No, no, no," I said. "Raya needs this now. She's
been looking forward to it for months. Kulich is only made

around Easter. Another time would be next year. Raya won't be in your class then."

The children were busy on little rugs and at tables, all working independently on projects of their choosing. Raya was seated at the life skills center. She was washing a rock that she had first scrubbed with soap. I wondered what skill this particular task was helping her develop.

The first cottonmouth appeared soon after Petra had died from a brain aneurysm. One minute she'd been going on about a headache, the next she was convulsing on the floor of our bathroom. She was naked. She'd been about to step into the shower. As I spoke to the 9-1-1 operator, I wrapped her in our bedsheet and lifted her onto the bed. I didn't want the paramedics to find her naked on our bathroom floor. Of course, I didn't imagine at the time that she was dying, that she would not be asking me later about details such as these—where was she when it happened, what was she wearing, did she foam at the mouth (yes).

I shot that first cottonmouth with a pistol I borrowed from my neighbor, Joe Herm. The first thing I hit was a koi. Its shimmering orange and white body floated up to the water's surface. There was blood. For some reason, I hadn't expected blood.

It took two more bullets to hit the snake. I didn't stop, though. I fired three more bullets. I might have shot every last bullet in the gun except Joe called my name over the fence. "Put the gun down, Lev."

The second cottonmouth appeared soon after I began dating Vicky. It was late at night, and Vicky was looking out my bedroom window, identifying planets in the night sky. I didn't ask to borrow a gun from Joe that time. I called a number I found on the Internet, and a half-hour later, a white pickup truck pulled into the driveway. It was almost midnight. A guy wearing a backwards baseball cap set up a black tube with a sticky paper inside it. Within twenty minutes, he had the snake in the back of his truck.

Vicky asked if the snake would be OK. "Sure," the man said. "Vegetable oil will unstick him. I'll let him loose in the bayou."

It didn't occur to me then that the snake could be Petra spying on me.

I asked Vicky to accompany me to the fish store, a gesture akin to gently unscrewing the cap off a water bottle on an airplane to regulate the pressure so that the water doesn't spray all over. She'd been getting impatient. *You're treating me like a prying stranger,* she'd texted. The other reason I invited Vicky along was that she owned two large ice chests that would be perfect for transporting the fish.

To show my appreciation, I brought her a box of sweets from the bakery.

"Did you make any of these?" she asked.

I pointed to the vatrushkas.

She bit into one and closed her eyes as she chewed. "This is why I keep you around," she said. "I might be willing to take a knife in the chest for this." She opened her eyes. "That was a stupid thing to say."

We drove to the fish store in silence, Vicky's hand squeezing my thigh. We bought seven koi to replace the six the snakes had consumed and the one I had shot four years earlier.

As we tipped the ice chests out, the fish plopped into the pond, their muscular bodies breaking through the water's surface like chunks of fruit into gelatin. "You don't think you're just enticing the snakes to stick around longer?" Vicky said.

I didn't tell her that was exactly what I had in mind.

She brought up the snake man again.

"They're all God's creatures," I said.

"They're monsters, those snakes."

"They're just hungry. Like the rest of us," I said.

That evening Raya and I sat by the pond and watched the fish, both new and old, swim their figure eights.

"I think maybe those snakes could be your mother and your sister," I said.

"Because they came when Katya died?" She smiled. "Then I guess that means it would be OK to let Prince Boo out. Katya and Mama wouldn't hurt him."

"Oh, no, Honey. I don't mean that they're not dangerous snakes. If Prince Boo scared them, they'd bite."

She looked confused.

"I'm not sure how to explain it," I said. "But think about it like this: The snakes are dangerous not because they're bad or evil but because they happen to have a very handy tool that helps them survive. They use their poison to capture food to eat. And they use it to defend themselves when they're threatened. If you were a snake, you'd do the same."

"But I wouldn't hurt Katya or Mama," she said. She looked like she might cry.

I put my arm around her. "They don't know you're you. They don't have human brains, those snakes. I just mean that I think they hold the spirits of Petra and Katya."

Raya thought for a while. "If they don't know we're us, then why are they here?"

I watched the snakes from my bedroom window. The moonlight made the pond's surface glitter, and the snakes were like two erasers wiping away the glitter. Petra would find her way back home after death if she could, but Katya? If she'd lived, she would have sent Raya and me postcards from all over the world, signed them "XOXO," shorthand for, *This is all I can offer you.*

I couldn't blame her one bit. I wasn't there for her when Petra died. Sure, she'd been vicious and wild, but she'd also been a girl dealing with tremendous pain. I'd let her stay out all night and come home in the mornings stinking of booze and cigarettes. I'd let her waste away until she was so thin, I was sickened by the sight of her. I didn't put up a fight.

When she left for college, I was relieved to see her go. When she didn't ask me to visit, I told myself it was OK to leave her alone. I told myself she needed space.

Katya's willingness to forgive me was what I was uncertain about as opposed to the possibility that she and her mother had been reincarnated by snakes. The idea would have fascinated (and saddened) Petra. Still, if anything could bring Katya back to me, perhaps it was death. Now that she was gone for good, I wanted to hold Katya in my arms and tell her I loved her.

Maybe death made the dead remorseful, too.

☾

Three days passed without sign of the snakes. I couldn't take my eyes off the pond. I stood by the kitchen window and stared while I washed dishes. I watched while I did my morning and evening stretches. As preposterous as it was, I imagined the cat had killed them. I gave Raya the third degree. No matter how many times she said she hadn't let the cat out, I wasn't satisfied.

Enraged, she picked up the little acrobat figurine Katya had bought her after the Cirque de Soleil show, and she threw it at me. There was a loud thud and the sprinkling of shards. She ran into her bedroom and slammed the door. I stared at the pieces on the floor.

When I'd told Raya what happened to Katya, she'd said, "That makes me sad. I love Katya." That simple.

"Me, too." I'd said, "It makes me terribly, terribly sad. It makes me so sad, that I may be kind of strange for a while. I'm apologizing in advance."

Raya had nodded. "People aren't always nice when they're sad, just like they aren't always nice when they're sleepy."

Raya wouldn't come out of her room at dinnertime. I tried her doorknob. It was locked. I sank down against the against Raya's door. Never had she locked me out of her room before. I didn't even know she knew how.

The next morning at Raya's school, I helped the children make kulich. One little girl whose name was Candace stared at me while she poured the melted butter slowly, slowly into the mixing bowl, dragging it out as long as possible so as not to relinquish the dough to another child.

Six children were crowded around the kulich-making

station. I sat across the table on a tiny chair I was afraid would collapse under my weight.

"You're splotchy," Candace said.

"I didn't sleep well."

She told me she was having a birthday party on Saturday with a piñata and a jumping castle. "I hope you come," she said.

Raya was soaking the raisins. She gave the girl the stink eye. "He's my daddy, not yours."

"Raya," I said. "That isn't nice."

Raya glared at me. "It's not as not-nice as blaming someone for something they didn't do. It's not as not-nice as shooting someone."

"Let's not talk about that right now," I said. "We're about ready to add the sour cream. Who wants to add the sour cream?"

All of the children but Raya raised their hands. Raya's eyes were like windows into a house on fire.

While the dough was rising, Agnes circled the children on the floor and they sang a song about feeding a rooster by a green apple tree. They added other animals to the feeding frenzy: a dog, a cat, a duck, a goat, a cow, and a bird.

I sponged the tables, swept the floor, and took out the garbage. I sat outside the classroom on a white bench that faced the children's vegetable garden. They were growing carrots, peas, and strawberries. Mixed in with the vegetables were snapdragons, pink and yellow, and marigolds the color of Katya's sneakers.

Vicky sent me a text: *I miss you.*

I typed back, *Sorry, I've been out of sorts. No snakes in three days.* She texted back, *I took care of it for you. Snake man.*

I imagined the cottonmouths' panic, stuck in those tubes, hauled down a bumpy road to God knows where. I felt as if I might vomit. I would have replenished the koi pond every week for the rest of my life.

Right there at the children's school, I called the snake guy and cursed him for trespassing and taking what was rightfully mine.

"Your girl called me. She was there," he said.

I imagined Raya pointing to the pond, a vengeful look on her face. "There they are! Take them away!"

Of course he meant Vicky. I hung up the phone. Two more texts appeared from Vicky: *Are you there? You OK?*

I didn't answer.

When it was time to divide the dough into baking molds, I got fussy with the kids. "No mixing it. No pressing on it. We want to divide it gently, gently."

One boy with worried eyes carefully sectioned off a piece of the dough and dropped it inside the mold, afraid to touch it any longer. Raya sectioned off the dough with a steady, confident hand. She placed the dough inside the mold and lifted her hands dramatically.

"Perfect," I said. She didn't look at me.

Candace shoved her dough into the mold roughly.

"You're ruining it," Raya said.

"She's never made kulich before," I said to Raya. "She's doing her best."

"You have to eat that one," Raya said. "You can't have mine."

"I don't want yours," Candace said. "And you're uninvited to my birthday party." She looked at me. "You're still invited."

☾

I put the kulich into the oven to bake just as the children went outside for afternoon recess. I joined Agnes on the porch. We watched the kids run around every which way like ants whose nest has been disturbed. Some of the children climbed trees. Some swung across monkey bars. Others dug in the sand. Raya climbed a swinging ladder and sat on the top rung, which was a good nine feet into the air. She looked off into the scraggly thicket beyond the fence. Beyond that was the bayou. Beyond the bayou was the ocean. I wondered if she was already dreaming about leaving.

When the kulich was almost done baking, Agnes chose Raya and Candace, of all the children in the class, to accompany me to the kitchen, which was in another building. Along the walk, Candace talked again about her birthday party.

"The jumping castle is going to be as big as this whole playground," she said.

"There are no jumping castles as big as this playground," Raya said.

"Are too. And so many balloons they'll fill up the sky."

"That's stupid," Raya said.

"Raya," I said. "We don't use that word."

Candace looked at me. "She called me stupid three times today. And she stole a puzzle piece from me."

"Did not," Raya said.

When we got to the kitchen, I put on a pair of striped oven mitts and removed the baking pan with the kulich from the oven. I set it on a trivet to cool. Both girls peered at the golden brown breads.

"Don't get too close," I said. "The pan is hot."

I crossed to the refrigerator and rummaged for the icing. My back was turned five seconds tops when someone screamed. I flung the door closed. It was Candace, and the first thing I felt was relief that it was not Raya.

I carried Candace to the sink and put her hand under cold running water. Still, she screamed. She carried on as if a shark had bitten her arm off. There was a red line across her fingers, but it wasn't anything serious. Her fingers would continue to sting for a half-hour or more, but soon enough, the pain would go away.

"You're going to be fine," I said.

I knew what had happened. It was the same as when I shot that koi after Petra died. It hadn't really been an accident. I'd seen the fish under the snake. I'd known I might hit it. I'd wanted to kill it. And I'd wanted to shoot the rest of them, every last one. Sometimes the pain is so great that all you can do to feel better is pass some of it on to someone or something else.

I told Candace she could pour the icing and the sprinkles both. "Raya doesn't get to do any of it?" Candace said.

Raya and I nodded. I'd whispered in her ear that we'd make kulich of our own, and she could cover the kulich in an entire container of sprinkles.

Candace grinned. She drizzled the icing slowly, slowly, just as she had done earlier. She took her time with the sprinkles, too.

"Beautiful," I said. "I've never seen more beautiful kulich."

"My hand still hurts really bad," Candace said.

"Then lick the icing bowl," I said. "That will make you feel better." I squeezed Raya's hand.

We watched Candace work a finger around the bowl in figure eights.

AN IMPROMPTU LESSON
ON BLACK HOLES

I have a habit of worrying about improbable outcomes. For instance, Nick packs our perishables for a camping trip in an ice chest along with two bags of ice, and I feel sure that the food will be room temperature by the time we back into our reserved camping spot; that the yogurt, cheese, sliced carrots, and deli meat will draw heat with the cunning of an alligator snapping turtle wriggling its wormy tongue to attract prey. To reassure myself, I reverse the scenario in my head: if I wanted the perishables Nick packed in ice to be room-temperature by the time we arrived, I could be certain I'd end up having to brush ice crystals from the ham.

I try the reversal now. Imagine he's a good guy, and I want him to find us, only we can't make a sound, can't show ourselves—we're in a black hole. How could he find us?

Especially if we are in danger because a bad man, a gunman (like a mythological chimera, only part man/part gun) is also coming for us. Yes, then I would think, the good guy will not find us in time.

It's not working.

Perhaps because our being found and killed is not an improbable outcome.

Four minutes now, and still I haven't heard the click of Sheila's heels against the tiles or her hand on the class-room doorknob, checking that I locked it. When Sheila announced the lockdown on the intercom, she neglected to use the words "drill" or "practice." An oversight. Our first drill has been on the calendar since the start of the school year three weeks earlier. (Three weeks, Sheila said during a planning meeting, should be enough time to acclimate the children to classroom routines, "to get them comfortable.") But the fact of the matter is this: if Sheila had said "drill," my legs wouldn't be shaking. I wouldn't be clenching them with the rigid determination of a person trying to hold in intestinal gas.

It was at the dinner table, Nick across from me—chew-ing, chewing, chewing—that I came up with this idea of black holes as a metaphor for lockdown drills.

Black holes aren't part of the kindergarten curriculum, and I won't teach the unit on space science until spring, after we study rocks and soil and other earthly phenomena. This impromptu lesson on black holes lends a new meaning to teaching to the test.

I told the children that black holes keep everything hidden inside them; that they could be bright as carnivals inside, but from the outside, all you see is darkness. Then, Alesha Sims, who at the age of six is the resident expert on everything, raised her hand and said, "Actually, light can get out, eventually."

I didn't argue. Her parents are scientists. Twice a month, they send over graduate students to conduct hands-on experiments with all the children in grades K–5. They've been doing this for two years, since Alesha's older brother, Ezra, started school. We didn't do lockdown drills then.

When I started teaching ten years earlier, after my younger daughter started kindergarten, the teacher who mentored me said that it takes six years to get to the point where you feel truly confident as a teacher. Six, she said, as though it was an indisputable fact: a price tag on a bottle of wine. I'd thought she was nuts. Then, my seventh year of teaching, I remembered, and I thought, yes.

Now I wonder if in six years I will be comfortable with lockdown drills. So far, I feel like I'm doing everything wrong. For instance: black hole?

I envisioned all of us hiding inside one black hole— together. The image in my head had been something like the time a parent brought a red parachute to class, and we'd all grabbed hold of the perimeter, pulling it down over our bodies so that the parachute plumped up like a fruit, and I'd said to the children that it was as though we were seeds inside the flesh of a tomato.

Five minutes since Sheila's announcement. The children, all twenty-three of them, stare at their shoes just as I suggested, so they won't get the giggles or forget to refrain from talking. Even Jeremiah and Julio, who are always arguing about whose turn it is to play with the magnets or the animal adaptations matching game. Even Tanya, who asks to go to the bathroom two dozen times a day. I can't even hear their breathing over the hum of the air conditioner. They have taken to the "activity" (not "drill"—too much explaining; not "game"—too fun) with such earnestness, it's as though they really aren't here.

Or: it's as though they are dead. Playing possum. Even among animals other than humans, for which most predatory behavior is a matter of necessity, predators aren't interested in already-dead prey. Of course, for most predators, this preference is judicious: fresh kills help ensure your meal doesn't make you sick.

I suppose we are also adapting a protective strategy similar to that of a school of fish or a herd of zebra the way we are wedged together in the cubby room. Safety in numbers: the rationale being that as an individual you're difficult to pick out from the crowd. Of course, for this method to be effective, we would need to be in motion. We would need opportunities for escape. In truth, we are more like fish caught together in a net.

But we are not "together" really. We are each an individual black hole, each of us alone.

Nineteen years of marriage now, and the evenings our teenage daughters are out with their friends or at extracurricular activities, Nick and I sit across from each other at the dinner table, and our communication often consists of a series of mundane questions: How was your day? Did you happen to make it to the post office? Do you want the rest of that Parmesan? We emit a string of one-word answers like microscopic photons thrown off our surfaces: fine, yes, no.

Each of my answers has a paired response, trapped inside it by nuclear forces. I feel them like lead balls in my core.

During our staff meeting about the lockdown drill, nobody raised the question of whether a gunman would be so easily fooled by a quiet building and locked doors when outside, the staff section of the parking lot is full of cars. Is he supposed to think we're all on a field trip?

Nick seems to be so easily fooled by my silence during dinners when the girls are out. If he suspects that I withhold, he doesn't let on. He takes what I give him. Then he clears the table.

Five and a half minutes. Like the children, I stare at my shoes. I've given myself a headache the way I used to at solo contests when I played clarinet in high school. Then, I was afraid of failure: missing a note, making the instrument squeak, public humiliation.

What I want is for Nick to notice my absence—to come looking for me, draw me out. Like we're playing hide-and-go-seek.

But it's as though my presence or absence makes no difference to him. Like he can't see me either way. Like no light gets in there, wherever he is. I wonder sometimes if he's no less hidden from himself than he is from me.

When we tried couples therapy a few years back, his body was in that plush blue chair with the brown paisley pillow, but his mouth put out scanty, depreciated words about how he loved me and wanted our marriage to work. More scattered photons. And afterwards, when I suggested we do our assigned homework—identify and compare our "love languages"—Nick didn't know what I was talking about. Homework? he said. Love languages? Like his input valve had been shut off even more than his output valve. Or: Maybe there's a barrier in his head that prevents input and output from mixing until he's ready. Like the reactants in a hot pack. They're inert until you break the barrier, and then comes the chemical reaction.

Nick isn't one for heat.

I try to draw him out sometimes. I wave my arms. I holler. I tell him how alone I feel.

He just shakes his head. He looks exhausted. I don't understand what you want, he says. I love you, he says. I'm a good man, I'm a good man, I'm a good man.

What he means is what he doesn't do. He doesn't stay out late drinking. He doesn't do coke. He doesn't crash his truck through backyard fences. He doesn't hit me.

Nick's father did all those things. He was a bucket emptier, to use the metaphor I teach the children to help them measure their feelings and how they treat each other. As in, when you pushed Robby, you spilled his bucket. When you helped Cara stand up when she fell, you filled her bucket.

Sometimes I think Nick's father shot holes in his bucket, that refilling it is impossible: The love just dribbles right back out.

Nick's father is why Nick is a black hole.

I guess I could blame my parents, too—for my being attracted to a man who hides from me, whose hiddenness drives me to hiding also. But where does that get me? Blame is how a man ends up massacring children and teachers at a school. Or: people in a movie theater or a mall or a political rally.

Do these gunmen blame the people they kill? Or: Are we just easy targets?

The way Nick was an easy target for his father.

The stories Nick has told me are heartbreakers. They have more than a little to do with why I fell in love with him in the first place. He knows what it's like to live in fear of terrible violence. He knows what it's like to hide and hope to God you're not found. He knows how to survive.

But that's the problem, really. He became too good at hiding.

And maybe I'm not one to talk. Nick is an easy target for me too. For my fear that I married too hastily. For my regret that I gave up grad school to have babies. That I watch too much television and don't exercise enough.

No one tells you that when you teach children, whether yours or someone else's, you will constantly come face-to-face with your hypocrisy. Like this bucket stuff. I've been talking to children about their buckets for years—teaching them how to fill their own buckets and the buckets of others. Fill others' buckets, I say, and you inadvertently fill your own.

The problem I don't address: how do you fill anybody's bucket when you're overflowing with resentment? Or fear?

I wonder now, what is the measure of the distance between Nick and me? What is the measure of the distance between us and these gunmen who take their resentments and fears out on innocent strangers?

Nick isn't a bad man, no. But does that make him a good man?

Am I a *good* woman?

Seven minutes. As much as I'm worried that the children will make a noise and that a gunman will find us and make us silent forever, I'm also suddenly worried that they will be silent forever whether or not a gunman comes. I'm worried that they will hide from themselves and from the people who love them.

I'm worried about the anger their fear will breed.

We're rehearsing for our deaths, after all. If the children didn't understand the gravity of what we're doing here in the cubby closet before, they surely grasp it now. Their teacher's legs are trembling as though a T. Rex is about to grab hold of her with its teeth. Their teacher puts her finger to her lips even though Tanya's tights are soaked, her neck red with shame.

There's no reversal to help me out here. Anger and fear are shackled together.

All I have is this: Despite everything, it's Nick I long for right now. I almost believe that I exert force enough to draw him here from wherever he is, no matter the distance or the magnitude of the forces keeping him away.

And this: what Alesha said about black holes, that eventually light will escape.

Once this drill ends, if this drill ends, I will spend the remainder of the day—and the school year, if it comes to that—drawing the children out of hiding. Tell us how you feel, I'll say. Tell us what you need.

THE NATURE OF LIGHT

They watch the planetarium's projection screen as the moon drifts silently over the proud eye of the sun, momentarily effacing it. She tells her two-year-old that the sun and moon are playing peekaboo.

Later, in the throng of people exiting, her husband is huddled so close that from her arms their son manages to press a hand behind each of their heads and push until they are cheek-to-cheek, then eye-to-eye.

"Mama and Daddy an ee-lipse," he says.

"Haha!" they both say uncomfortably.

"Pretend!" their son demands.

"Who is eclipsing whom?" she asks. Her husband starts to open his mouth, but with her one free eye she gives him a look.

"No!" their son says. "Pretend you *one* ee-lipse."

Their son is interested in their proximity, not in who is obliterating whom.

What she thinks about on their walk home as the sun wanders off, leaving the moon hovering blindly now like an iris faded by cataract, is how the light illuminating this scene is over eight minutes old. If the sun were to be extinguished for real, no one would know it until eight minutes after. She and her husband and son could be strolling along a downtown sidewalk just like this one. In eight minutes, they could place every animal their son knows onto Old Mac Donald's farm.

But eight minutes is nothing. The light from the second-nearest star, Proxima Centauri, is 4.2 *years* old. The light from the Orion nebula, the belt buckle of the only constellation her husband can identify—over 1,300 years old. The most distant light humans can see with the naked eye—two and a half *million* years old. For all anyone knew, the Andromeda galaxy could have burned out long before humans gave a name to it.

When did they stop going out to the lake? In those early years, they used to chase each other up and down the slopes between the trees. Every day was a series of hot, hungry breaths. The way she remembers it, only sleep could knock them loose.

Now the mundane routine of sleeping side by side often seems all that clings.

All those congenial eyes in the sky winking down at them, they're not what they seem. They're snapshots in an album, telling a story of what was.

She read somewhere once that couples who display photographs of themselves together throughout their homes are more likely to remain together. The light from what was can sustain love, it seems, keep it generating. Of course, it's also true that relationships can drag on mirthlessly, scraping by off travel-weary light from love that expired long ago.

You wouldn't think it could be impossible to know whether the source of a light still exists. You wouldn't think one could search day after day and come up with so much contradictory evidence. Light is murky.

If theirs is no longer breathing, how long until they will see it with our own eyes? Until they see the light snuffed out?

TAXIDERMY Q&A

I didn't plan to put my foot out in front of the city bus tire. I'd been angry, and I just did it. It was spontaneous. In a way, it was an accident. My leg broke free of my mind, and I was too late to stop it.

I'd been working at Laurel's Lair for about two months. I was a trainee. There was no guarantee I would eventually become a dominatrix. Mostly I followed the lead of whomever I was working with. Often that was Laurel herself.

There was much I wasn't allowed to do yet, so I mostly glared and laughed and said mean things to the men. This was what they paid for, so I didn't feel bad about it.

And I thought I was good at my job, that perhaps I showed talent.

On this particular day, Laurel said I could take the lead, and she would assist and observe me. She chose this client because it was a fairly simply job. All he wanted was to be humiliated—no pain, no instruments.

"What could go wrong?" she said. "You make him crawl around on the floor. You tell him how pathetic he is. A piece of cake."

As usual, we began by gagging him with a white strip of cloth. They liked that. Then I told him to crawl like a baby and to rub himself against the cold, concrete floor. We laughed at him.

But something seemed wrong. When he crawled, there was haughtiness in the graceful movement of his legs, the way he carried his torso long and proud. Every chance he got, he looked me straight in the eye, as if challenging me. He was like a cat rubbing past me, only to turn on me in pity, as if my need for him was all too apparent.

I had to do something. I had already planned my ascent into the dominatrix world, and this jerk wasn't going to stop me.

So I pulled the cloth out of his mouth and said, "What's your problem, you little piece of shit?"

He said, "I'm pathetic."

"Yes," I said. "You are pathetic. You're worthless. You're a miserable little maggot. Say so."

"I'm a miserable little maggot," he said, but he seemed to be smiling at me, as if he was going to make fun of me later to his friends.

"Now sing, 'Itsy Bitsy Spider' and show us just how miserably pathetic you are," I said.

"I'm so pitiful that I don't remember how it goes."

"Well, then I'll teach you, you sorry, little fuck." I began reciting the words to him.

Laurel cut in and said, "I think the little maggot is lying. Let's teach him a lesson for lying to us." She gagged him again and pushed him onto the floor. She told him to put his legs over his head to form a human pretzel.

When the session was over and the client gone, Laurel yelled at me. "You never give the client control. What on earth were you thinking, Sylvie? You were supposed to humiliate him, not yourself."

I left before Laurel could fire me. When I got to the bus station, I stood near the curb, intentionally inhaling the exhaust fumes. The bus would be so crowded and hot and dirty. I just knew I'd have a nervous breakdown. But my bag was heavy, and it was a long walk home. I couldn't decide.

When the bus began rolling, I shot my foot out in front of the back tire. I swear I hardly knew what I was doing. I was just so angry—at myself, at Laurel, at that man, at the people in the bus station. It was like the time I threw my xylophone mallets in high school. Mr. Gapinski stopped the piece because of me. It was the fastest, most technical sequence in *The Lord of the Rings*. It was damn near impossible. I was practicing three to four hours a day and I couldn't get it. He yelled at me in front of everyone, and the next thing I knew, I'd thrown the mallets. One of them hit a flute player named Marjorie in the head. The other bounced off the director's stand and fell at his feet. I walked out of practice and never went back.

Dear Chester

Q: I have a cape with ticks all over it—seems like hundreds. I put it in the freezer for twelve hours and when I checked on it, it was as if they'd actually multiplied. Most of them aren't moving, but a few are. And if they're alive, I'm afraid the others might be as well. There's a whole militia of them. Should I go ahead and pickle it? Will that kill them? I don't want them getting loose and taking over my garage. Then I'll never get rid of them. I'm in a real jam here. Can you help me?

A: Keep doing what you're doing. Freeze them. Freeze them for a good four or five days. That ought to do the job. I've taken a cape out of the freezer after two days and found those suckers

*still crawling around, but after four or five days, not a one
will be breathing.*

*You might try pickling, I guess. Probably they will drown
in it, but I like freezing myself. You're sure to wipe them out.*

The thing about the taxidermy question-and-answer seg-
ment of the *Nimset Gazette* is that it makes me feel weak
and animal, as if my gut is spread open, organs exposed.
But in a good way. I imagine this ripping apart is the beginning of something extraordinary.

Maybe I won't always be a failure. Maybe it doesn't matter that I couldn't make it as a dominatrix, that I'm not even
good at being cruel.

So what if for the rest of my life I'll be carrying around
a foot that looks like a mangled, fatty piece of chicken, the
bit you cut off and throw away?

I imagine that I can be repaired, made new again, made
into something unrecognizable.

These people, mostly men, write letters detailing their
taxidermy problems and crises. They reveal their slips, toils,
flops, botches, and fiascoes without shame. They say, I've
gotten myself into a scrape. They say, I'm driven from pillar
to post. They say, up the creek, up a tree, run aground, and
in a spot.

Some of them haven't failed yet. Some of them are just
beginning. And they say so. And they ask for help. They
say, Do you have any suggestions? Can you point me in the
right direction? Can you teach a young dog some tricks?
They are so open and frank, my heart flutters.

The best part is that their questions are answered by a
man named Chester: Chester the Hero, Chester the Savior,
Chester the Great. He knows everything there is to know

about the preparation, stuffing, and mounting of the skins of animals. And a whole lot more. He consoles and teaches these men. He is kind and warm. He is the person you want to be team captain. He would never pick you last. He would embrace everyone the other captain left behind.

What I love about Chester is his optimism. The man circulates optimism like a bad cold, like campaign buttons, like the Book of Mormon. But it's optimism, and it is so precious. And he wants to share it with you. He makes you think you can do it. He wants you to be successful. He says, Don't sweat it; stick in there; good luck, buddy.

It's beautiful. It's cathartic. It's hallelujah, praise the Lord.

Dear Chester

Q: I'm new to this, and I have a set of artificial deer antlers that need fixing. It's a clean break, so I thought about using Super Glue, but I wanted to know what you think. A friend gave them to me, and they're too nice to throw out. Can you give an amateur a helping hand?

A: You repair them the same as real antlers. Find the center of the antler pieces and drill a hole about an inch or so deep in each. Make the hole in both pieces just slightly larger than your threaded rod. Bondo in a piece of threaded rod into one of the holes. Once the rod is firmly Bondo'd in, try matching the pieces together by inserting the other piece onto the opposite end of the rod. If it doesn't match, you may need to bend the rod a little or make the hole bigger. Mix up some more Bondo. Then hold the pieces together until hard. Trim the excess.

Super Glue might hold them together for now, but I wouldn't trust it. You want something that's going to last, something that you can be proud of. Good luck, buddy.

For a while, my hurt foot meant I could sit around and feel sorry for myself. I'd fractured more bones than you want to know. Nurses grimaced in pain and disgust for me, though they tried to hide the latter. They cleaned my dreadful foot and cared for it. They said kind things. My roommate Anna brought me my favorite foods the entire time I was in the hospital. We watched *Beauty and the Beast* and *The Elephant Man*, in honor of my foot, she said. And I loved her for it.

Truth was, Anna was all I had.

I met Anna in the bathroom of an STD clinic. There hadn't been any toilet paper in my stall, so I'd asked her for some. Then she'd asked if I'd been to the clinic before. I lied. She said it was her first time, too. She was there because her boyfriend found out his ex-girlfriend had herpes. I was there because I'm paranoid, and STD clinics are one of the few relatively safe ways I know of to get a high. Of course, it's a gamble, but one of the few gambles I've repeatedly lucked out on.

Waiting for the results was wild. I would diagnose myself with every STD out there. I read up on them. I planned my future around them. I came to accept them in a way that made them not so bad, even AIDS. I was prepared, and preparation was important.

The best part, the reason I kept going back to STD clinics, was receiving the results. Finding out I didn't have any of those awful diseases was euphoria. It meant I was safe for a while, that there was something I'd beaten.

While we washed our hands in the clinic bathroom, Anna told me she was scared. She was already sure the test would be positive. She and her boyfriend had fought over this and now he was her ex-boyfriend. He'd moved out of the apartment. She'd moved to Seattle with him, and she hardly knew anyone else in town. She was lonely, and she couldn't afford her rent. She asked if I might move in with her.

I said, "I've been looking for a roommate myself. Rent's so expensive."

Money wasn't the problem, though. I had a job as an assistant manager in a toy store at the time. I also knew that I could always get cash from my parents, that all I had to do was say the word and sleek checks would arrive wrapped in blank paper, disguised as letters.

Really, I was just lonely, too. I went out sometimes with coworkers, but mostly I stayed home and read self-help books. I'd read them all. *How to Think Positive. How to Quiet the Critic Within. How to Hug Yourself.* I'd even thought about writing one of my own—*How to Beat the Shit Out of Yourself: When Discipline Is Necessary.*

Anna seemed so sweet, and she was pretty in a non-threatening way, and who didn't like that? And she was a musician, a composer, actually. She'd composed the scores for several small-budget horror films. There'd been *Turnstile Massacre, A Turkey Nightmare,* and *Wife Number Five.*

I'd thought that some of her talent or luck, whatever it was, would rub off onto me. I didn't know what I wanted to do exactly. I wanted a calling.

When I began working at Laurel's Lair, Anna hadn't approved.

"I don't think there's anything wrong with it. I just don't think *you* should do it. I think it can really mess a person up. I think you're too sensitive. I mean that in a good way."

Dear Chester

Q: I have a deer skull I'd like to bleach and preserve. It was bur-
ied and is stained a dark brown. Is there a way to whiten
and preserve it, or is it too late?

A: It's never too late. Find yourself a beauty supply store
and get some peroxide used for bleaching hair. There are
two parts—a cream lotion and a powder. Mix it accord-
ing to the directions on the package; then brush it onto the
skulls with a paintbrush, preferably an inch or two wide
to make your job easier and faster. BE SURE TO WEAR
RUBBER GLOVES!
    Then bag the skull in plastic overnight. The next day, rinse
with cold water. If it's white enough to suit you, then hang
it to air dry for a few days. If not, try another treatment or
two. You can seal it afterwards with clear lacquer. It will stay
white forever.

I followed Anna out here to this little hunting town in the
pit of the Midwest because she won the house on a game
show. She didn't care what kind of a town this was or who
lived here as long as it was cheap and she got some work
done. And when she invited me, I thought, a free house,
why not?

When we got here and found out how small Nimset was,
that it was inhabited mostly by men who hunt, and that the
weather dropped to below zero with the wind chill, I felt
cheated.

"We should have known," I said. "Nobody ever wins anything good on that show."

"Nobody's forcing you to be here," she said.

Since the swelling in my foot had gone down, Anna had stopped feeling sorry for me.

I think she thought I would feel better after the move, that I just needed some fresh air, a change of scenery. But I felt worse. I didn't know what to do with myself, and watching Anna work hard day after day only made my depression worse

"Why don't you do something? All you do is complain," Anna said.

"Are you kidding? This is jubilee city. This is a rocket ride to ecstasy," I said.

Anna ignored me.

I propped my bare feet on the table, crossing my bad foot over my good foot. This annoyed Anna, I knew, but she wasn't going to let on that it did, mainly because she didn't want to hear about it anymore. I'd say I was still in pain, and she'd want to call bullshit.

This had become our routine for the last few weeks: her being pissed off about my foot, me being pissed off about her music.

All Anna did was work all day, and she wouldn't let me hear it. She took her keyboard outside every morning and brought it in late at night. She wore headphones. She said she was onto something and that she couldn't share it with me just now. She moved with this dreamy, determined look on her face. She tapped and she hummed, and she closed her eyes. I thought of my mother.

I'd told my parents that I wouldn't be giving them my new number. I told them I needed to move on with my life, that I needed to break the ties that bind me. It's what they each told me just five months earlier when the divorce was finalized and the phone calls began.

They had one-track minds. They called to brag about their new lovers and how great their lives were now.

I couldn't care less about the divorce. Good riddance to that, but the details they told me. It was enough to drive you batty. My father called me once to talk about Charlene and what a looker she was. "You have to admit it, Sylvie. She's a good couple of notches above your mother. Charlene is feminine. She cares about how she looks. She shaves her legs every day. She doesn't let herself go like your mother did. She has better taste than your mother, too. You should see what she's done to the house. It's like living in the god-damn Metropolitan. She is first class, honey."

To his credit, Charlene was the only woman he's seen since the divorce. In fact, she's the same woman he was seeing before the divorce.

Mom, on the other hand, was on her way to having a fling for every year she wasted married to my father. There'd been Hank and Dean and Ned and Spike and at least a few others, whose names I couldn't remember. She called to tell me how handy they were, how smart, how artistic, how strong. She said things like, "Always check a man's hands before you sleep with him, Sylvie. Beautiful hands are next to godliness."

I liked to think that comments like that were invitations to tell her about me for a while. I would start to say something, but the phone would go silent—not an I'm-giving-you-all-of-my-attention kind of a silence, but an I've-got-things-to-do-and-this-isn't-what-I-called-for kind of silence. That's how it's always been with her. If I did bother to really say something to her, she would say, *Sorry, Sylvie, something's come up.* She'd say, *My brain hurts, and I just can't handle having this stupid phone pressed against my ear right now.*

What pushed me to my limit with the phone calls was her calling me in the middle of sex with Spike just so I could hear the quality of her orgasm. I picked up the phone and heard gasping and screaming, and the first thing I thought was that I was overhearing a murder. I wondered who it could be. Was it someone I knew? And was the caller the victim or the murderer? There was something exciting about a murderer calling me every time he made a kill, sharing such an intimate, dangerous thing with me. If only I could have something that intense, I wouldn't care if it was with a murderer.

Then my mother said, "Did you hear that, pumpkin? Your mother hasn't screamed like that since before you were born, Sylvie. You can testify to that, can't you, pumpkin? You never heard anything like that coming from our house when you were growing up. No, sirree."

I wanted to think my parents were using me as a go-between, that they hoped I would carry the news on to the other one. But I was afraid it wasn't that at all, that it was really me they were each talking to. I was their freak. They took one look at me, and they felt better about themselves.

My parents did ask about me when I hurt my foot. "How did it happen?" they asked. When I told them it was run over by a bus, they were silent.

"It was a terrible day," I said. "First I lost my job, then this. I was on my way to being a dominatrix."

"Oh," they said. They asked whether I could afford the medical bills. They each sent checks. My father's checks had a picture of a bear sipping out of a stream. My mother's checks had a Navajo design in pastels.

Dear Chester

Q: I'm a beginner and have been mostly using videos. I have a frozen whitetail cape that a friend gave to me, and I want to flesh, pickle, and tan him. I'm hoping to make a decent mount of him. I turned the ears, split the lips, tubed out the nose, and cleaned the eyes. Should I salt and pickle next? Or flesh first? I've seen it both ways in the videos, but which is the best? Thanks, man.

A: Flesh it. Some will say to pickle it for twenty-four hours, then shave it. But I always flesh, then pickle, then shave. I've never done it any other way. I guess I can't say for sure what is best, but I've never had a complaint, and I've been doing it this way for over twenty years. But I reckon it's up to you. Let me know how it turns out.

When Anna came inside the house to make a drink before returning to work, I put on my blue balaclava and made my hand into a gun and said, "Hey, lady, give me all your talent."

Anna said she didn't like it when I talked like that. She said it wasn't true, that I had as much talent as she did. "Not everybody can stomach hanging a man by his balls and then spitting on him until he cries."

She knew I hadn't really been a dom, but she'd believed me when I told her that Laurel let me do those things, that she let me because I was good, because I showed a lot of promise.

"I'm just messing with you," Anna said.

Yes, we're just clowning around, just making sport, just shooting the shit.

"You know I love you," she said.

"You're my one real friend," I said.

"Me, too. We've got nobody but each other."

Truth was Anna had five siblings. She had a family who sent her letters just to send letters. On her birthday, she got at least eight cards, and no dinky Hallmark cards either. Her cards were all handmade. They had a rule in her family that it wasn't worth anything unless you made it yourself.

I thought that was the greatest thing I've ever heard. Anna played it down, though. She said her parents made up that rule because they were poor growing up. She said it was a trick to make them feel good about wearing home-sewn clothes, that it was nothing special, just an act of necessity, of survival.

"You're going to be OK, you know. It could have been a lot worse. You could have had to have your foot amputated," she said.

Sometimes Anna was too much to take, like the princess sugarplum sister I never had. Even in the red balaclava she worked in, she had eyes like something from deep under the ocean, something that had never seen the light of day. They made you wish that you could be from there, too.

"Don't give me any ideas," I said.

"You say a lot of stupid things," she said.

I wondered if Anna knew me well enough to know I'd done it on purpose. I wonder if she knew I'd thought about doing other such things before—plucking out my eyelashes, cutting words into the flesh of my hip, dipping my finger into the garbage disposal.

I said, "I'm going to go out and find me a real hunter man. I'm going to ask him to get me a chipmunk to put on the coffee table."

"You're being mean."

Maybe I was, but I knew there were a lot of people out there with terrible secrets. And they all wanted to be repaired, even if they couldn't say so. And to be repaired, they first had to be punished. That's why some went to a dominatrix. It had nothing whatsoever to do with sex.

I decided I'd suffered enough. I was going to meet Chester, and he was going to make everything OK. I was going to let him fix me up and make me beautiful.

Dear Chester

Q: I've mounted two whitetail deer so far. The first was a ramshackle, but I was pleased enough just having completed it. With the second, I wanted to do better. It seemed to be going pretty well, beautifully even, but now it's all falling apart. The problem is the ear cartilage. It's not sticking to the earliners like it's supposed to. I want the ears to lay back. Should I try Bondo on them? Or do I need to remove the cartilage? Help!

A: If you try Bondo with the cartilage still attached, chances are you're going to have the same problem. The ears are not going to cooperate. You'll save yourself some hassle and frustration if you just remove the cartilage. It'll give you more control. Use a good quality earliner and rough it up some first. Then add some Epo-Grip epoxy and set your ears. This will take care of those stubborn ears and whip them into place.

The newspaper provided Chester's full name, Chester D. Banks, so I looked him up in the phone book. And sure enough, there he was. He had two numbers and addresses, one next to his name, then another underneath it, next to the listing, "taxidermist/barber."

Since he was only about ten blocks away, I walked. I could walk on my foot quite well. It was a little crooked, still bruised, and all of my toenails, or those that remained anyhow, were black, but it worked.

I dragged it a bit, though. Anyone could see how pitiful it was, that it shouldn't have to carry all my weight. It was still my hurt foot, and sometimes I thought it would hurt forever. And I kind of liked that. It was something to count on, something that couldn't be taken away from me.

I wore sunglasses so that I didn't have to think about what to do when I saw people, whether to look at them or away. I looked wherever I wanted, and what they saw was me tall and swift, gliding between their bodies like they were branches, and I the fifty-foot woman. They would not forget me. I was something this town had never seen. All of my failures were the prelude to my success, the promise of it.

There was a wooden sign hanging outside Chester's shop. The words "taxidermist" and "barber" were burned into it, and it seemed that it couldn't have been any other way. Chester made things by hand, too.

Inside, a man sat in a dark green barber chair, and behind him was a sink and a large mirror. At the far end of the building, there were several long wooden countertops. They were mostly clean and clear, but for several boxes, buckets, two mounted deer heads, and some tools laid out as if for surgery. On the walls were pictures of nature scenes torn out of calendars and several child drawings of red and purple stick figures with unnaturally large heads with big mouths that seemed to be smiling or screaming.

The man in the chair wore a flannel hunting jacket like Anna's, similar pattern of greens and blues. He had messy brown hair that fell into his eyes in a way I thought was sexy. He looked to be about thirty or so, much younger than I'd expected. He had an intensity about him.

"Chester," I said. "My name's Sylvie. I wanted to meet you."

"Nice to meet you, Sylvie." He stood and gave my hand a squeeze the way you might to assure a loved one. And it worked. I felt assured.

"I'm here because I read your column," I said.

"Oh, that. You have something that needs stuffing?" He smiled.

Just then, a door in back opened and in walked an older man with the round, pink face of a cherub, except that the cherub face was at war with a much harder face, one dented and marred from exhaustion.

"What can I do for you?" he said.

I turned back toward the younger man who was watching me closely. I felt foolish, yet I still preferred the younger Chester and didn't want a switch in players.

"Are you the Chester who writes the taxidermy column?" I asked the older man.

"That's me." He gave the younger man a stern, knowing look. "Is he bothering you?"

"No. I just assumed he was you."

"Well, Paul's not me. He's just a joker who needs a haircut."

Paul winked at me and sat down.

"Like I said, what can I do for you?" Chester washed his hands in the sink behind Paul with blue dishwashing soap. A couple of bubbles escaped from the plastic bottle, only to collapse when they collided with their reflections in the mirror. He rinsed a comb, squeezed a dab of soap onto it, too.

"I just love your column," I said. "It's so full of hope."

"What's that?" He spritzed Paul's hair with water and combed it.

"Hope," I said. "Optimism." I had imagined he would know me somehow, like no one else ever had. Look at me, I thought. See me, please.

"Did you say you just wanted a little bit off the ends? Then shave the bottom?" he asked Paul.

"Precisely," Paul said. He did something goofy then with his eyes. He moved them this way and that frantically, and then winked at me again.

"Not many people around here are really interested in taxidermy. They come to me for that. Most of those questions I make up myself. Nobody reads my column," Chester said.

"I read your column," Paul said, leaning his head back to grin at Chester.

"Shut your trap." Chester pushed Paul's head forward.

I was surprised by his confession, but that he made those questions up made me like him even more.

"Well, you're wrong. I read your column and whether you make up the questions or not, I think it's the most wonderful thing ever. Really," I said. I wanted to reassure him. Maybe he needed repair, too. Maybe we could help each other.

"That's kind of you," Chester said. He parted Paul's hair.

I smiled. "I came by because I think you can help me."

"Uh-huh," he said. "What kind of a problem do you have? If you bring it in, I'll have a look at it."

"Oh, I don't have any deer capes or anything like that. I just want to talk to you. I just—."

"If you have a taxidermy problem, I can help you. Otherwise, I think you've come to the wrong place."

"I think you're wrong," I said. "I think you're underestimating yourself."

"Chester's always underestimating himself," Paul said.

Chester gave him a knock on the head with the comb.

"Please help me," I said. I was scared I would walk out of there with nothing. And then I didn't know what I'd do. "I'm a mess. I'm a disaster. Just look at my foot." I held it out toward him. "I did this to myself. It wasn't an accident."

Chester glanced at my foot. His face was stone cold. He turned back to Paul's head and continued cutting. "You did that to yourself, and you want me to fix it."

"Yes. I don't know."

He tossed the comb and the scissors into the sink. He plugged in an electric razor, tested it, and then turned it off.

"You're just like Jenny," he said. "I bring her daisies, and she lops off their petals with my hangnail scissors and pokes pencils through their yellow centers, which she calls faces. And then she tells me she can't help it, that it's something I did to her. She's eight years old."

"What? This isn't like that." I stepped back a tiny bit.

"It's exactly like that. All this crap about how you can't help it. I have to help you. It's all about you. You never hear a man talk like that."

"That's not true at all," I said.

Chester switched the razor on again, and Paul leaped from his chair.

"You're not touching me with that. You sound crazy as hell, man," he said.

Couldn't he see what state I was in? I couldn't imagine how anyone could be so insensitive, so terrible, and I said so. "You're a terrible person. Terrible, terrible."

Chester's cherub face looked more like a radish now, purple and bitter, and he looked as though he might really kill one of us. "Get the hell out," he said.

Paul ran out of there, and I followed.

Paul and I went to a bar just down the street called Orson's Well. It was round and made of brick and had a chimney at the center. The bar was dark, lit only by the fire and very dim ceiling lamps over every other table. There were no windows at all. The tables were unfinished and rough and had benches like picnic tables. Despite the fire, it was quite cold inside, like being inside a cave.

I ordered a double shot of whiskey and Coke. Paul ordered the same and the second round in advance.

I momentarily panicked when I realized there was no corner for us to sit in. When Anna and I went out and found that the corners were occupied, we waited for a corner to open up or we went elsewhere.

"There should be corners for everyone," she'd once said.

"No," I'd said. "Not for everyone. Just us."

The outer tables were cut so that they fit along the curve of the brick wall, and if I couldn't have a corner, I was at least going to have a wall. Paul and I sat down, and we looked at each other above the rims of our glasses as we knocked the first one back.

He wiped his mouth and said, "You're crazy talking to a man like that when he has a razor next to another man's head."

"I used to be a dominatrix," I said. "I'm used to dealing with crazy men."

"Oh, yeah? Do you have a whip?"

"No. I don't do that anymore."

"That's too bad." He knocked down his second drink.

"Why?" I said. "Do you want to take me home with you?"

"Well, maybe."

"Is it my foot? Because if it is, that's stupid. It's just a foot. I can throw a sock on it."

"What happened to it?"

"Nothing," I said. I finished my second drink and said that I was going to get another. He asked me to get him two more and to tell the bartender to start him a tab. Before another fifteen minutes had passed, we'd drunk those as well, and he got up to order another round.

"You look like somebody," he said. "I don't know her name, but I saw her in a movie once. She was pretty funny."

"But the point is you don't remember her name, and she was only in one movie. She's a loser," I said.

"But she was very funny."

"Then why don't you want to take me home? Am I not funny enough? I can be funny."

"I think I do want to take you home." He knocked back drink six. "Yes, I think I do."

I called Anna. She was frantic.

"Where have you been? It's getting dark."

"I've gone out and met people, and I won't be coming home tonight," I said.

"Please don't do that, Sylvie. You're drunk. Let me come get you. Where are you?"

"Orson's Well. But you can't. I met me a man. He thinks I'm funny."

"I'm coming to get you. I'll be there in a few minutes."

I grabbed Paul by the arm and told him we had to go.

"What's your rush? We're hanging out."

"Listen," I said. "If you want to take me home with you, you have to do it now."

"You sure are being pushy. Fine. Let's go then." He settled the bill, and he took off out the door, practically dragging me behind him.

Outside, snow was falling. Several inches had already accumulated. I zipped my coat and shielded my eyes with my hands.

"Well, look at that," Paul said. "Makes you proud to be an American." He sang the national anthem at the top of his lungs, his hand over his heart.

The sky was a fuzzy blend of purple and gray and orange, and it made me think of my stomach. I was going to be sick. I moved over to the ditch and puked my guts out, and in the snow, my vomit looked like something that had died. I sat down and held my hair back in case it happened again.

Paul had moved on without me and was half a block away. A woman was walking towards him, and I realized it was Anna.

Paul stopped singing and asked her if she was an American.

She tried to ignore him. He asked his question again.

"Yes, I'm an American," she said.

"Then why don't you hold your hand over your heart? Are you not happy with all that this great country has given you? Do you take all this for granted? Do you think you deserve better? Are you ungrateful?"

"I'm just on my way to meet a friend," Anna said. She hadn't noticed me yet.

"Woman," he said. "Put your hand over your heart and sing with me."

She tried to move past him, but he grabbed her by the arm. I knew he was acting crazy, but I was jealous anyway. I wished it were my arm he was grabbing. I mean it would have been my arm if she hadn't come out looking for me and if I hadn't drunk too much and gotten sick. Or even better, she could have seen him holding me like that and together we could have fought him off, and she and I would have gone home arm in arm and stayed up all night talking in the kitchen. And then I would have stopped complaining about my foot, and she would have let me listen to what she'd been composing. And we would have been happy.

He took her other arm and pressed it into her chest. "Come on now," he said. "If you don't know the words, I'll help you. After me. Oh say can you see."

"Oh say can you see," she mouthed. Then she saw me. She yelled my name.

"Louder," he said. "By the dawn's early light."

"What have you done to Sylvie?" she said.

"Sylvie? I haven't done a thing to Sylvie. Now sing with me." And he jerked her arm so hard that her body seemed to flap after it like a flag in the wind.

She yelled my name again, and I wanted to help her, I really did, but I felt so weak. I had a hurt foot, and I just didn't think I could stand on it. I felt that if I tried to stand, I might fall right back down and hurt something else. And anyhow, Anna would be OK. Paul would let go of her any minute. He just wanted a song. It was only the national anthem. And it was a good night for it. The falling snow looked like the embers of a nuclear disaster. And the orange purple haze, it looked like the throat of a screaming mouth.

KINETIC THEORY

In college, my only friend was a long-limbed boy named Kaleb. He had a habit of rearranging other people's things.

Sometimes I caught him in the act. I'd watch him move the books on my shelf so that some were vertical, others horizontal. If I asked why, he'd say something like, "I can't believe you didn't notice how miserable they were."

Other times I'd discover his work after the fact. I'd look up and find that he'd spun the postcards on my wall into a fractal or that he'd organized the food in my mini fridge by density. When I asked when he'd done it, he'd shrug. "We both know you're not particularly present."

It was true. I had a habit of disintegrating. I drifted nebulously like a cloud—changing volume, changing shape. I bumped into people on the way to classes. Whenever a door closed, parts of me got left behind.

If I had to guess why Kaleb hung out with me, I would say it was because he could rearrange me, too. If he told me a dress wasn't flattering, I'd get rid of it. I'd wear whatever he picked out. If the next week, he wanted to pierce the auricle of my ear, I'd guzzle vodka, grit my teeth, and present my profile.

And when Saturday night rolled around, I accompanied Kaleb to whichever gay club he chose. I hoisted myself up into a cage five feet off the ground and imagined that the bars could contain me. Inside those bars, there was just room enough for one body to dance. Two bodies and what you were doing was something else. Kaleb said that dancing like I did, a skinny girl alone in a cage, made me look tragic. Every Saturday night, I spooled myself inside the music until I was wrapped so tight in its sticky web that my heart knocked against my ribs.

We drank before we went out—tequila, tequila, and more tequila. I sweated the alcohol off dancing so that I was screeching sober by the end of the night.

Kaleb usually found a boy in leather pants to yoke himself to. Their rhinestone collars would shimmer in the club's harsh red lights, and pressed together, they'd look like a red-winged blackbird on the hinge of flying away.

But sometimes Kaleb would push through the gyrating bodies to make his way toward me. He'd say, "Come down," and I'd lower myself from the platform, and he'd lace his fingers through mine and lure me between bodies until I was engulfed by heat. Then, just as I felt myself expanding, rising, he'd put his hot hands on my face and reel me in until he was kissing me on the lips, his tongue in my mouth.

He kissed me like this in his dorm room, too, sometimes, when we'd been talking about the boys who'd broken Kaleb's heart. He'd pin me on the floor, and my chest would become as compact as the contents of a suitcase.

After, Kaleb would sit back and laugh. "You think I'm a good kisser?" Or "Aren't my lips the perfect combination of soft and hard?" Or "Did I make you wet, Ellen, honey? Come on, you can tell me."

At the club, no matter how the boy Kaleb had picked up that night twisted and turned in the dark, always when the strobe light caught him again, the expression on his face was the same, as though he wanted to pry me open like an egg, see what was in there.

The hospital smell of baby powder spraying out of vents, the techno beat poking at the soles of my combat boots, Kaleb's tongue poking at my teeth: these forces felt like they were all that was keeping me from scattering all the way out to Earth's exosphere, where particles are still bound by Earth's gravity but too ethereal to collide.

STORIES PEOPLE TELL

Kate waited for Finlay to invite her to sit on his crummy sofa, and then he did. He patted the cushion next to him. "Com'ere," he said. He flipped on the television, to a program called *Real-Life Horror Stories*. The "f" was a dagger dripping blood. "You ever watch this? People talk about some fucked-up shit. The kind of stuff that happens in movies, the kind of stuff you forget happens in real life," he said.

He placed his arm around Kate's shoulder and kissed her neck. No question in his mind why she'd come over. She, on the other hand, hadn't been sure what to expect. The first few times she'd hung out with Tommy Tucker, he hadn't laid a hand on her.

The woman on the television recounted how she'd barely escaped death on a shopping mall escalator. Kate laughed at first. They both did. Death and disaster on a shopping mall escalator? It was ridiculous.

But the woman's eyes became wide and haunted as she recalled how the escalator started moving so fast that people fell as they were trying to step off and so in no time at all, people were piled on top of one another. "Like pieces flying off an assembly line," she said. People became trapped. A baby was smothered under its own mother's weight. Body parts were shredded in the escalator's teeth, including the storyteller's arm. If she normally wore a prosthetic, she did not for the show. Her left arm ended in a stump at about the height of her breast.

"My friend Stacy has a prosthetic leg," Kate whispered. "From a horse-riding accident."

"Oh, yeah? How high up does it go?" He tugged at her nipple with his teeth, right through her shirt and her bra. She shrieked.

"Just above her knee."

"Too bad." Finlay grinned at her, and though she didn't quite understand, she knew it had something to do with sex. She grinned back.

Kate had taken her mother's car to Finlay's trailer. She had her driver's permit. Technically, she wasn't supposed to drive without a licensed driver accompanying her, but her parents were visiting her little brother in juvie and weren't expected back for four hours or so. If they beat her home, she'd deal with the consequences later.

When Finlay had opened the door, Kate had been confused, then disappointed. At the club the weekend before, she'd thought he'd had a certain astral quality, as though he'd materialized out of one of the mirrored disco globes reflecting the club lights in every direction. When she'd thought about him, which had pretty much been every second of the past six and a half days, she'd pictured him in a moonlit clearing in a forest, the wind mussing his hair.

Still, he wasn't ugly exactly. He was trim, and his lips weren't chapped the way Tommy Tucker's lips had been when she'd made out with him. Like kissing a scab.

The important thing was that Finlay was a man, the real deal. Twenty-two, or so he'd said. Now she wondered if he'd shaved a few years off. Not too many years. He was wearing a surf T-shirt and ragged jeans, after all. His hair fell to his earlobes, in which were embedded gold-brown buttons the size of ibuprofen tablets. Tiger's eye. But there was a pile of mail on the table with his name on it. He groaned about needing to oil the front door of the trailer to fix the squeak.

She couldn't fault him for lying, not when she'd claimed to be eighteen. It made them kind of even.

The woman on the television said she'd thought she would never step onto an escalator again and that for a couple of years she didn't. "But then I was running through the airport, desperate not to miss my flight, and I did it. I think I held my breath the whole way up. But it wasn't so scary after that. Now I take them all the time. The nightmares haven't gone away, but you have to live your life, I guess."

By the time Finlay unzipped Kate's jeans, the escalator story had run its course, and a second woman began telling a story, about being held at gunpoint in the middle of the day in a sales office she'd worked in. The guys with the guns bound her and her coworkers' wrists and ankles with duct tape. They shot one guy in the kneecap when he tried to overtake them. They shot and killed a dog. The woman's boss had brought the animal to work. She remembered being relieved when they shot the dog. "The darn thing wouldn't stop barking. Seemed like it was either going to be the dog or it was going to be the rest of us. Better the dog."

After it was all over, the woman didn't leave her house for two weeks. She didn't want her boyfriend to leave the house, either. She didn't want to be alone. Her mother had to bring them groceries. But then, as was the case with the woman who told the escalator story, she eventually moved on with her life. She went back outside. She returned to work.

Finlay's mouth on her underwear, Kate closed her eyes. She froze for only a moment. Then her body went limp in submission. She'd felt something like this with Tommy, but she'd known with him that she would let it go only so far. For starters, that was before she'd begun taking the pill, and she'd been so dumb as to believe that oral sex offered protection from STDs as much as from pregnancy, that it was safe to let him put his mouth anywhere he wanted and for her to put her mouth on him as long as they didn't put their genitals together. So, so stupid. She saw that now, and she blushed to think of it. But also she didn't want her first time having intercourse (real sex, she had called it) to be with some clumsy, overly eager boy who came before she'd even felt anything.

"God, I want you," Finlay whispered into her thigh. She moaned then, and the sound startled her. It was authentic, spontaneous, not a sound she'd manufactured for a laugh. She could hardly believe it had come from her body.

On the television, a man told about the time he and his younger brother hitchhiked home from a carnival. The driver didn't speak a word to them, wouldn't answer their questions, wouldn't stop when they pointed out various locations they'd like to be dropped off at. He just kept driving. The man sounded scared as he spoke. He sounded old, too. Sixty? He was remembering something that had happened to him longer ago than Kate's mother had been alive, but still he was shaken. Of course, the show's producers had told him to play up the drama, to make the story scary. But his fear didn't seem fabricated. And this was *his* story he was telling. It really happened to him.

Finlay pulled away from Kate, and she waited, her eyes still closed, for him to return. But he announced he was out of beer.

"That's OK," she said.

"That's so not OK."

When she opened her eyes, he was standing by the door, jiggling his keys.

"I thought," she started to say, but stopped.

He grinned. "For after. I don't want to have to get dressed and go out for it. It'll just take a few minutes. There's a store real close."

Outside, she noticed the Dumpster, from which protruded three lumpy bags of garbage. They looked like the rumps of ducks fishing under water. Next to the Dumpster sat a green sofa and on it lay a gray cat.

"Look, it's napping," she said.

"I'm pretty sure it's dead. It hasn't moved in three days."

"Poor kitty."

They drove to a convenience store that had two gas pumps, both with orange poster board signs taped over them reading, "$ Only. Pay First."

Inside, Kate lingered by the candy as Finlay picked out beer. She worried that if she stood with him, the clerk might not want to sell to him on account of her being underage. She didn't want to cause trouble for him. She didn't want to have to drive to another store.

A girl a little bit older than her entered the store and asked the clerk for a pack of cigarettes. She wore short shorts and a little black camisole. Her blonde hair was pulled up to expose half her back. Kate was relieved she couldn't see Finlay's face as he stood in line behind the girl.

The girl gave Kate a dismissive look as she left the store as if to say, *What are you looking at, fuckface?* Kate quickly turned away.

"Ready?" Finlay said after he paid.

The girl with the cigarettes was long gone, and Kate was relieved to be alone with Finlay again. When they climbed into the truck, she leaped toward him and kissed him full on the mouth.

He grinned. "Oh, yeah?"

He used his left hand to steer the truck, while he devoted his right hand to trying to unbutton Kate's jeans. As they entered the trailer park, he cursed at the difficulty of the task. He looked down at his fingers, and Kate looked, too. She watched the delicate bones moving beneath his skin, thought about how they looked like piano keys. She'd taken lessons up until the age of thirteen.

Neither of them saw the little girl on the purple bicycle. She was five or six maybe, and she and the bicycle were lying on their sides on the asphalt on Kate's side of the truck when Finlay slammed his brakes and yanked back his hand.

Kate gasped. She buttoned her jeans.

☾

When Kate climbed out of the truck, the slow spinning of the bicycle's front tire came to a stop.

The girl was breathing, the only visible injuries a scraped knee and palm, but the look in her eyes was wild. The kind of look that made you want to turn around and check behind you, the kind of look that gave you the shivers even though you were just sitting on a sofa watching television and there was no reason to think you were in danger. Kate thought the girl must have hit her head, that when she lifted it, there would be blood, brains maybe. What if she fell onto a nail?

"Oh, God! Are you okay?!" Kate said.

The little girl wasn't looking at Kate, though. Her eyes were on Finlay, who was now standing in front of the truck. He looked incredibly calm.

The little girl hoisted herself up slowly. Then she said, "You hit me! You hit me!"

If there was any damage to her head, it wasn't obvious, but brain damage wasn't always obvious. Kate had read a short story for English class in which a boy was hit by a car, got up and walked home like everything was fine, and then a few days later, the boy died.

"Don't you know you should look both ways before crossing the street?" Finlay said, a little too callously in Kate's opinion. After all, this was a very little girl, and she'd been riding her bicycle in a trailer park, not on the street, and holy shit, she could have died, might die still.

Only a few lousy streamers hung from the bicycle's handlebars. Most of them were nubs. They'd been lost long ago, probably by a previous owner. The bike looked like it had been dug out of a Dumpster. Why these details should make Kate sad when there were far worse things to think about right then, she didn't know.

The girl said, "You're supposed to stop for people in the road!" Then she started crying, wailing actually, as though her intent were to draw attention.

Kate pictured herself and Finlay cuffed in the back seat of a squad car. She didn't know anything about him.

He had a good chin, though, sharp like a razor's edge. And his fingers, well, she had never noticed anyone's fingers before, but she noticed his, their exquisite shape, as though they'd been carved from wood, the most beautiful fingers she'd ever seen.

And he had made her feel something she'd never felt before. The way that moan had escaped from her body without her knowing it was going to happen.

Kate helped the girl to her feet and walked her a few steps away from the truck. Finlay picked up the bicycle and followed.

"You're OK," Kate said. "Just a few small scrapes."

"He almost killed me."

"Now, wait a minute here," Finlay said.

"Shh," Kate said to both of them. She patted the girl's hair. She pulled a tissue from her purse and dabbed the girl's cheeks and eyes. "You're fine. You're going to be fine." In all likelihood, it was true.

A figure came running from several trailers over—a woman, about the same age as Finlay maybe. When the girl saw, she ran to meet her.

"Qué pasó? Qué pasó?" The woman looked back and forth among all three of them.

"He hit me with his truck!" the girl said. She wrapped her arms around the woman's plump thighs.

"Look," Finlay said. "It was an accident. She looked like she was waiting for me to pass. I had slowed down, you see, and was about to stop, but she was stock still, waiting, and so I went, but then just as I did, she pulled out into the street all of a sudden. I slammed on my brakes. I did all I could given the circumstances. She's lucky I only barely clipped her front tire. She should be more careful."

Kate was shocked to hear him lie with such ease. He could have stopped with "It was an accident." He could have simply said, "I didn't see her," and he wouldn't have been lying at all.

At the same time, she was impressed by his steadiness. He was handling the situation, cleaning up the mess, like her parents had when someone broke into their home when they were away on vacation a few years back. Kate and her little brother had been afraid to sleep in their own beds after that. But her parents had been so cool. They'd swept up the broken glass, filed an insurance claim, allowed Kate and her brother to sleep with them for two nights only, just until the security door was installed, then insisted that they be brave.

"April!" the woman said. "You could be hurt, mija! You don't go into road when there's car."

"He wasn't watching!" the girl said. "He was looking at her!" She pointed to Kate.

The woman looked at them for a moment, then back at the girl. "It doesn't matter what they do. You pretend cars don't see you!"

"Imagine," the girl said. "Imagine, not pretend."

Finlay looked to Kate. He set his hand gently, but firmly, onto her shoulder. She felt his warmth, heard his words in her head, *God, I want you.*

"Tell her," he said to Kate. "Tell her what happened."

Kate looked back and forth between Finlay and the girl. Then she said, "April, you gave mixed signals when you stopped like you did, like you were waiting for us to go. You really do have to be much more careful."

The girl's eyes widened again. For some reason, she hadn't seemed surprised by Finlay's lie, but she was by Kate's. Kate could see this plainly.

But the woman was right. April should have assumed they didn't see her. She should have waited. You never trust a driver is going to stop for you. Never.

On some level, Kate hadn't needed to add anything more, except she'd needed to demonstrate her allegiance to Finlay, of course. But it wasn't just that. She'd needed to distinguish herself from the girl, to show what side of the line she stood on.

Now the woman would take the girl home and wash and bandage her knee and hand. Maybe she'd give her some ice cream or a snack cake. She'd run her fingers through the girl's hair and tell her she was going to be just fine, and for a little while at least, the girl probably would be.

Kate would return to Finlay's trailer. They'd resume their places in front of the television, on which the old man's face was frozen in mid-speech, his mouth open, black inside there. She'd find out what happens next.

VIRGINS

The summer Meredith Goobis lost her virginity, Star was eight years old. She'd known Meredith only a few days before it happened. She met her at church camp, which Star and her brother, Harris, ended up at because their grandma Myrna said she was fed up watching them all day long every day June, July, and August. She had stuff she wanted to do, she said, though everyone knew full well that gossiping on the telephone, working crossword puzzles, and reading trashy romance novels were all things she could just as easily do and did do when Star and Harris were in her care. Still, she wasn't paid anything to watch them, so when she said it was about time they got a religious education and that she knew for a fact that Bayou Baptist, her church, charged less tuition than any other summer care in town, less than their mama probably spent on wine in a given year, the matter was settled. Their dad would drop them off at church in the mornings. Their grandma Myrna would retrieve them at two in the afternoons and keep them until their mama could pick them up after work.

Meredith's mother, Mrs. Goobis, was the teacher for the sevens and eights. She had the round, mottled face of a cauliflower.

That first morning, she led the children in the pledge of allegiance to the American flag and, seemingly, the Texas flag, which stood pompously beside its more discreet companion. Then she taught them a verse: "My brethren, count it all joy when you fall into various trials, knowing that the testing of your faith produces patience."

She offered a translation: "That means ya'll will experience many troubles in your lives, but instead of being sad or angry, you should be happy. By giving you trouble, God tests your faith in him. As your faith grows stronger, you'll learn patience."

"Patience for what?" Star asked. Before church camp, all Star had known about God had come from her grandma Myrna, and mostly what she taught was that you should constantly pray for what you wanted, no matter how trivial, because if you didn't have the foresight to do this, your life would consist of an endless series of irritations. Think long lines at grocery stores, dogs yapping day and night, television programs that don't record when they're supposed to, corns on your feet aching even when you wear the most comfortable of shoes.

Mrs. Goobis frowned. "We raise our hands and wait to be called," she said to the room of children sitting cross-legged in a circle. The rug they sat on was a dingy pattern of browns and oranges. The walls of the classroom were covered in wood paneling from which all manner of ghoulish faces stared out.

Mrs. Goobis stared at Star. Star stared back, thinking the teacher was formulating a response to her question about patience.

A furry-eyebrowed girl with tight ringlets of coppery hair and cheeks the color of raw beef turned to her and said, "Mommy is waiting for you to raise your hand."

Star never would have guessed the girl had grown in Mrs. Goobis's belly. She was the spitting image of her father, who'd been the church's organist before he took off and left his family, Star's grandma would later tell her. Nobody, not even his own mother, knew where he'd gone.

"Star," Mrs. Goobis said when she raised her hand.

"Patience for what?" she repeated.

"Why, patience that your faith will be rewarded."

Star raised her hand again. "Like the suicide bombers getting thousands of virgins in paradise?"

She'd heard this on the radio in her dad's car. The men who'd flown into the World Trade Center and the Pentagon had believed that after death, God would reward them in paradise with seventy-two virgins apiece and that each of those seventy-two virgins would be attended by another seventy-two virgins and that they too would belong to the same man. Star didn't know what made words like girls or women insufficient, but she knew that whatever virgins were, seventy-two multiplied by seventy-two was a lot of them. She'd pictured her grandpa Gene pulling off the top of a sardine tin to find rows of little women stuffed inside. The women wriggled their shoulders and hips to try to make room. They grunted and groaned and pinched each other. In each woman's tiny fist was another sardine can, and these cans rattled as the even smaller women inside them squirmed.

Now Mrs. Goobis's face turned the color of her daughter's cheeks. She cleared her throat. "Those people, they're not Christians." Then, "Heaven is a place where your troubles are taken away forever."

Mrs. Goobis fingered the gold cross pendant around her neck. "But you have to have faith and patience. Take the story of God asking Abraham to sacrifice his only son, Isaac. Now, life doesn't get much worse than that. But Abraham trusted God, knew he was a good God and that he must have his reasons. Abraham did as God commanded. He took his son out to the mountain God had chosen. He was heartbroken, for sure, but he was prepared to do as God had asked. Then, just as he was about to take his son's life, God stopped him. He explained that he'd just been testing Abraham's faith."

When their mama came that afternoon to pick them up, Harris was watching a PBS program about supernovas and said he just had to see the end of it.

Their grandma Myrna barely lifted her eyes from her book to say hello. The book's cover showed a bare-shouldered woman with long, flowing hair. A man lurked in the shadows behind her.

Their grandpa Gene sat next to the kitchen window, his eyes squeezed shut.

In a white bucket next to his chair were two crabs. Since retiring the previous year, he spent a lot of time fishing and crabbing along the Texas City dike. Usually, he didn't catch anything.

The crabs tapped and scraped their claws against the inside of the bucket while a pot of water heated to a boil on the stove. Their grandpa meant to put the crabs into the water alive. Star was plotting how to save them.

Their mama asked their grandpa if he was all right.

"I'm telling that dog yapping away next door to calm down and shut its trap," he said.

Their mama said nothing at first. Her pants, which had

looked neat and smooth that morning, now sagged around her bottom. Her blouse had sweat stains. She fixed herself a glass of iced water and jiggled the ice so that it sounded like the crabs, like it too was trying to escape.

"How are you doing that exactly?" she asked finally. She stood in the opening between the dining area and the living room, where Star and Harris sat on the stiff carpet in front of the television.

"With my mind," he said, without opening his eyes. "I'm concentrating on the dog. I'm picturing it in my head—its scrawny body, its mangy brown fur. I'm telling it everything is OK, there's no need to bark, and it should go lie down and enjoy the sunshine."

"What makes you think this is going to work?"

"It works," was all he said.

So far it hadn't, though.

"How long does it take? To calm a dog with your mind?"

"It depends. It's all about focus and concentration, and you've just about destroyed mine with all your goddamn questions." With that, he opened his eyes.

"Sorry," she said. "Kids?" She turned so quickly toward the living room it was as though her body were connected to their grandpa's eyelids like some kind of Rube Goldberg machine.

"Five more minutes," Harris said.

"You're a scientist," their grandpa said. "You know thoughts are energy. When you think, you literally send energy out into the world."

"I'm not a scientist." Star's mama's job was to write science questions for tests for kids all the way from kindergarten up through high school. She'd written some of the questions Star had had to answer in the second grade, questions such as *What pattern does the sun make in the sky?* and *How do animals sense their environments?*

Now, Star wanted to know, did Grandpa Gene not know that crabs have senses? Did he not know that they have nerves just like him?

"You know what I mean," he said.

"So what if thoughts involve energy transfer? What does that have to do with this? By your rationale, can I lift a two-ton truck with my mind if I just focus on it?"

Star's grandpa slapped the table and stood up. "I would have thought you of all people would understand." He bent over and lifted the blue-speckled crabs from the bucket. Their core bodies were about the size of a generous slice of bread, but with their legs and claws extended, they looked like they could manage the steering wheel of a car. He held them away from his body, as if he might come after Star's mama with them.

Star bolted for the kitchen, taking the back way past the hall bathroom and the pea-green refrigerator. She stood between her grandpa and the pot of boiling water. "Please! They're living things! They feel pain!"

"I've had just about enough. Elizabeth, you come get this kid of yours out of my way."

"Can't you wait a few minutes?" her mama said. "We're just about to leave."

Her grandpa stood there facing Star and the pot, his arms outstretched with the crabs, like some kind of monster.

"One minute," he said.

Star's mama put her arm around her and walked her around her grandpa and out of the kitchen. They'd barely stepped from the linoleum to the dining room carpet when there was a splash and the click of the lid against the pot. Star screamed.

Her mama said, "For Christ's sake, Gene, what's wrong with you?"

Star was so hot that night that before bed she turned her ceiling fan on high and lay naked on the floor of her bedroom to cool off. When she went to sleep, she forgot to turn the ceiling fan back low again as her mama had instructed when they'd come home from the pet store with her hamster, Willie Nelson. He couldn't tolerate the temperature getting too cold.

The next morning, Willie Nelson was as hard as the ground after a frost. This was not how sacrifice was supposed to work. The story she'd told herself about the crabs was that though they had suffered, something good might come of it other than her grandpa Gene enjoying a meal out of them. She'd thought of the virgins in paradise.

She imagined they lived in a place like Pirate's Cove along the Gulf Freeway just off the exit for her town. The building was shaped like a ship, complete with pink barnacles, and after Star begged to go there for dinner one evening, imagining the waiters would be dressed like pirates and the booths shaped like boats, her mama had said, "Honey, there aren't any pirates, just a bunch of naked women dancing on tables. It's not for little kids."

"Who *is* it for?" Star had asked.

"Men," she'd said, at which point Star's dad had started to object, but her mama said, "I won't lie to my children."

Star pictured a backdrop with an image of the ocean, cardboard palm trees, and the aroma of coconut tanning lotion spraying out of vents. Everywhere women danced naked atop tables littered with drinks containing little umbrellas. The women had to step gingerly to avoid toppling drinks.

Her grandpa sat in a beach chair and watched them. He wore a Hawaiian print shirt and huge bug-eye sunglasses.

But what did the virgins want? Star wondered. Clothes? A break from dancing? Let the sacrifice of the crabs bring something good to the virgins in paradise, she'd wished.

What she got was a dead Willie.

She carried Willie into the kitchen in a blue handkerchief and set him next to her plate of scrambled eggs and toast, which she didn't touch. Willie lay there with his limbs sprawled out just like those of the iridescent green June beetle displayed in a little wooden box she'd bought at a garage sale. It occurred to her for the first time that the beetle probably hadn't died of completely natural causes either.

Her mama acted as though there was still a chance Willie might be OK. She said she'd take him to the veterinarian while their dad dropped them off at church camp. Star knew she was just trying to make her feel better, though.

In the church bathroom, as she and Meredith washed their hands, Star said, "Is that story about Abraham true?"

"It's in the Bible."

"It's terrible."

"That's blasphemy."

Star said, "Do all problems really go away once you're in heaven?"

Star started to turn the water off, but Meredith objected. "You can't possibly have sung all the way through your ABCs twice already."

Meredith yanked out four paper towels, one right after another.

"Heaven is whatever you want it to be."

"For everyone?"

"For everyone who goes to heaven. I'm going to have trees made of chocolate cake. I'll be able to go into a toy store and point to everything I want, and it'll be mine."

"Do animals go to heaven?" It made Star feel better to think that Willie was somewhere far, far away, enjoying a pile of hamster pellets.

She dried her own hands, wiping them on her jeans to try to make up for Meredith's excess paper towel use.

Meredith frowned at this. "That's unladylike." Then, "Animals don't believe in God."

Meredith pulled a shimmery blue container about the size of a large gumball from her dress pocket and held it out for Star to see. Inside was a tiny porcupine ballerina in a pink tutu. The ballerina twirled around and around. "I suppose animals could be in heaven if you want them there. Maybe I'll ask for a real dancing porcupine."

That past year, in the second grade, Star had written a story about a girl named June Beetle, who went to the zoo, but as she moved from one exhibit to another, no animals were to be found. At the end of the story, the girl left the zoo having seen nothing but rocks and concrete and all manner of barriers. Star's teacher, Ms. Sidney, had said she wondered what happened to the animals. "Now *that* could be a story," she'd said. So Star had rewritten the ending so that the snake was in its exhibit and it was the size of a house because it had eaten all of the other animals at the zoo. Their bones were piled around the snake.

"Doesn't sound like much of a heaven for the porcupine," Star said to Meredith now.

☾

That afternoon, Star lifted the Virgin Mary from the manger scene in her grandma Myrna's Christmas corner and studied her.

Her grandma's holiday decorations were on year-round display to forego the trouble of hauling boxes in and out of the attic all year long.

The lurid Technicolor figurines in the manger scene could just as easily have been part of the Halloween display. The mouths of the three lambs and the Virgin Mary were a curious red as though they'd been feasting on flesh.

"Why is she called the Virgin Mary?"

Her grandma didn't hesitate. "Because God, not a man, put Jesus in her belly."

"So a virgin is someone who's pregnant with God's baby?"

Her grandma thought, then said, "A virgin is someone who is pure and innocent."

"That's what Mrs. Goobis said about lambs and about Jesus. They make good sacrifices because they're innocent." Mrs. Goobis had also said that sacrifice was like a payment: the more expensive the thing you wanted to buy, the higher the price you had to pay.

"It's a different kind of innocence."

"So are you a virgin if you haven't had a baby with a man?"

"Something like that." She disappeared into the kitchen to make pork chops for dinner. If Star's grandpa Gene caught anything that day, it would have to go into the freezer, her grandma said, because she wasn't about to wait a second longer.

Star pictured her grandpa out on the dike, wiggling his fishing pole in the water. She could see him so well in her mind—his pale blue fishing hat pulled low over his eyes, tackle and hooks dangling from the brown band wrapped around it; the rough leather watch he still wore though it smelled like toe fuzz; the top button of his white shirt undone, tufts of hair creeping out like tentacles. She thought then about what Mrs. Goobis had said about sacrifices being like payments for something you wanted and what her grandpa had said about thoughts having energy, and while she hated at that moment to credit her grandpa with anything, if he was right and if Mrs. Goobis was right, then she might as well use her thought energy to trade her grandpa for Willie. She concentrated on Willie Nelson coming back from the dead and her grandpa Gene taking his place.

When their mama picked them up that afternoon, she said, "Good news, Sweet potato! Willie Nelson's OK! The vet said it was a rare condition, some kind of temporary paralysis. Willie's good as new now!" Star was skeptical, but she ran to his cage as soon they pulled into the driveway. There he was with his strange red eye (the other one brown), his teeth chomping down on hamster pellets.

She didn't buy that temporary paralysis thing for a second. What other explanation was there but that she had brought him back to life with her mind?

But then she remembered her grandpa. Had he and Willie really changed places? Was this what Mrs. Goobis had meant when she said that everyone has God inside them?

Just before morning recess the next day, a woman brought in a platter of watermelon slices and cookies. The students were directed to take no more than two cookies and two slices of watermelon, but Star watched Meredith Goobis slip an extra couple of cookies into the pocket of her white eyelet dress. They weren't well concealed in that pocket full of pin holes, but no one else seemed to notice, so Star shoved two extra cookies into the front pockets of her shorts, one onto the front of each thigh.

They were then sent outside to the playground. "Go on, go," Mrs. Goobis said.

On the playground, Star watched Meredith take off for a steel tunnel that burrowed through a grassy hill. She followed her at a distance. Meredith crawled in and settled with her back to the church.

The boys from Star's class picked up sticks and pretended to shoot each other. The other girls sat in a neat little row, each braiding the hair of the girl in front of her. After several minutes of this, the girl in back moved up to the front of the line, rested her hands on her knees, closed her eyes, and smiled.

Star squatted at the opening of the tunnel. Meredith's hand moved from her dress to her mouth. Star wondered if Meredith didn't have much food at home. Her mama was forever talking about how lucky they were to have plenty of food to eat, a roof over their heads, and money to take vacations.

"You want mine, too?" Star said.

"What are you talking about?" Meredith snapped her head around. She wiped the chocolate from her lips with the back of her hand.

"I saw you take extra cookies," Star said.

"I did no such thing."

"I took extra, too. You can have them if you want."

Meredith eyed Star suspiciously. "How do I know you're not going to tell on me?"

"I guess you have to have faith."

Meredith considered this. "You have to have faith in God and your parents. The Lord didn't say nothing about having faith in other kids."

"Suit yourself."

Meredith put her palm out then. Star placed one cookie in it, then the other.

"I brought my hamster back to life from the dead," Star said.

Meredith ate a bite of cookie. She said nothing.

"I did it with my mind."

Meredith finished chewing and said matter-of-factly, "Only God can bring a dead animal back to life."

"Well, I guess this just proves I have God inside me." Star tried not to think about her grandpa, torn apart by a shark.

Meredith looked at Star the way people often looked at Tony Green, the boy in her second-grade class who wore eyeglasses so thick they magnified his eyes to the size of golf balls and whose khaki pants were always coming unzipped, his penis popping out like a cuckoo bird from a clock. Sometimes he'd chased her around the playground, calling "Twinkle, Twinkle! Twinkle, Twinkle!"

"That's sacrilege. Now come here," Meredith said.

Star inched her way into the tunnel. She sat down against the lukewarm steel, gritty with sand. It was ninety degrees outside already, and humid, but here in the morning shade, the air wasn't so bad yet.

"Open your mouth, little lamb," Meredith said.

"What?"

"I'm going to feed the lamb as Jesus has asked me."

Star thought that perhaps it was Meredith who was crazy like Tony Green. "What are you going to do to me?"

"Trust me."

Star reluctantly opened her mouth.

Meredith did not spit into her mouth as she'd feared. She didn't fling sand. Meredith held up the last of the cookies and placed it gently onto Star's lower lip. Although the cookie was the same variety she'd eaten earlier back inside the church, it tasted sweeter and richer now, when the hand offering it was not her own. Meredith offered her another bite and then another until the cookie was gone and Meredith's fingers pressed against her lips. Star felt a strange pulsing then in the place where her pee came out. *Vagina* was the word her mama used. Her grandma Myrna called it a *hoohoo*. Star had never heard her dad or her grandpa Gene speak of it one way or another.

Meredith said, "Jesus *is* inside you, Star. You just have to listen."

What Meredith seemed to mean, as far as Star could tell, was that Jesus was saying yoo-hoo from her hoohoo. Her hoohoo seemed like a peculiar place from which Jesus might speak, but then again, maybe this was precisely why her grandma Myrna called it her most sacred place.

Star's grandpa Gene did return home the day Willie Nelson rose from the dead, but the next afternoon he was not himself. His body crumpled over the dining table like a yellowing plant. He ate a piece of dry toast.

"What's wrong with Grandpa?" Star whispered.

"His back. The pain killers haven't taken effect yet. That old man acts like he's still in his forties. It's no wonder he's not worse off than he is."

Star noticed the black toenail on his right foot and how it dangled from the skin beneath by a tiny thread. Toenails weren't like baby teeth. Her grandpa wasn't losing his toenail so that a larger one could grow in. The most logical explanation for that toenail and his crumpled posture was that he was dying.

After her grandpa went back to bed to rest his back, her grandma Myrna spent the afternoon gossiping on the telephone. She talked about how foolish this one was, how pitiful that one was, and how ugly another one was. Star could hardly hear a word from the television, and to make matters worse, when Star's back was turned, her grandma snuck chocolates into her mouth without offering her or Harris any. All that nasty gossip and those chocolates and the heat made Star want to smother her with her dingy old peach-colored armchair pillow.

When her grandma hung up the phone for the third time that afternoon, Star said, "I could kill you with my mind."

"What did you say?" Her grandma pushed her glasses higher up on her nose and looked down at Star.

"Grandpa's dying because I was so angry with him for taking the lives of those crabs and then Willie Nelson. I focused on Willie coming back and Grandpa taking his place, and now here we are."

Harris turned around and shook his head like their mama did when she said someone was a lost cause.

"It's true!" Star said.

"Child," her grandma said. "What kind of foolishness has gotten into you?"

But Star didn't stop. She told her just what she thought of her nasty old gossip and her stupid books and her being stingy with her chocolates.

On the car ride home, her mama said that what she'd said was hurtful and that Grandpa Gene was most definitely not dying. She let out a big sigh as they got out of the car to pick up burritos for dinner.

The next morning Star learned she was no longer welcome at her grandparents' house, not for a few weeks at least. She would have to go to Aunt Constance's in the afternoons, which meant Harris would, too, since it was too much of a pain for their mama to have to pick them up at different locations.

Aunt Constance had four kids, so her house was always loud. Plus, the oldest kid, Walt, was twelve years old and loved to torment Harris. Harris called him the Human Garbage Disposal because he had an affinity for funky meat products like Vienna sausages and Spam.

"Nice work," Harris said to her.

It was a few days later that Meredith "lost her innocence" as Star overheard one of the teachers say about it later.

Meredith had been in the restroom an unusually long time, and Mrs. Goobis sent Star to fetch her. Star passed two other classrooms along the way. Through the window of one door she saw the fives and sixes crowded around a red puppet stage. On it danced a white-robed figure, presumably Jesus, his hair long and wavy as Star imagined Meredith's hair looked in the mornings before her mother got to it. Through the window of the second classroom, she saw older kids rolling around the floor laughing.

When she opened the door to the girls' bathroom, she thought she'd chosen the wrong door. The shoes within the only shut stall were not those of a young girl. Large black sneakers nearly the size of her dad's shoes was what she saw. They were facing the toilet. Star was leaning against the bathroom door, ready to get out of there quick, when she saw the little red Mary Janes dangling above the black shoes like ornaments from a tree. She was a little girl, Meredith, several inches shorter than Star, and Star's own feet only barely scraped the floor when she used the church toilets.

She thought, Meredith passed out, and someone is giving her CPR. She thought, crazily, Meredith fell in, and he's pulling her out.

She called Meredith's name.

There was a barely audible, "Shit." Soon the door to the stall opened, releasing energy in an explosive burst the way tectonic plates do when they push past each other. The boy, a teenager she guessed from his height, gave her a quick, guilty look as he whisked past her. His cheeks looked hot to the touch. Then he was out the door.

Star found Meredith sitting on the toilet as though on an ordinary chair, her skirt neatly laid out over her knees. She ran the back of one hand across her mouth. With the other hand, she held a Barbie doll dressed in a bright, sapphire blue gown that sparkled. She held it up as though it were a prize she'd won.

"Your mother sent me for you," Star said.

Meredith asked Star to hold the doll for her while she washed her hands. She cupped water into her hands, swished it around her mouth, and spit.

Star watched her. She didn't know what she had seen, but she had a bad feeling about it.

"You want some juice?" Star asked.

Meredith nodded, so Star led her to the kitchen where they helped themselves to apple juice that had a grainy texture as though the skins had been ground up into it.

☾

The next day, neither Meredith nor Mrs. Goobis was at church camp.

Star didn't hear the new teacher Mrs. Fox read or explain the verse for the day. Her mind was on Meredith. That Meredith was no longer eligible to become one of the virgins in heaven was little consolation for her having a baby. Star wanted Meredith's innocence to be returned to her somehow. She pictured her lying in a field of colorful wildflowers. She said to her there, *Relax, everything's OK. Feel the sunshine on your face.*

For three days she concentrated her thoughts on making Meredith OK again. She squeezed her eyes shut and saw little supernovas going off in her head like fireworks. She drank gallons of water, and every time she peed, she listened for the voice of Jesus. What she got was a headache and a swashing feeling in her stomach as if she were carrying around a miniature ocean.

It was her grandma Myrna who took her to see Meredith. Her wood-paneled Chrysler careened into the driveway, kicking up dust and rocks. She said simply, "That girl could use a friend right now," and she handed Star a Tupperware container of strawberry muffins when she climbed into the back seat. Her grandma didn't say a word during the drive to Meredith's, not even when they passed the highway billboard sign for Pirate's Cove, which boasted "All-You-Can-Eat Ribs for $7.99," and which normally elicited some word of condemnation from her. If she heard Willie Nelson scratching around in Star's backpack, she didn't let on.

Mrs. Goobis answered the door in a night shirt that ended just above her knees. It read, "I don't do mornings" and featured a cat with rollers in its fur, bunny slippers concealing its front paws. She held a piece of jerky in her hand. Her eyes were vacant. Star wondered whether Mrs. Goobis even saw her standing there with her grandma.

Once they were in the house, Star's grandma put her arm around Mrs. Goobis, and she motioned Star toward the hallway to find Meredith. It wasn't difficult. The door to her room advertised itself as such in pink wooden letters.

Star knocked on the door expecting that she wouldn't answer or that even if she did she'd be in a similar state as her mother—vacant and nibbling jerky.

But Meredith beamed and said, "Star! Mommy didn't tell me you were coming over for a playdate!" Star had been right about Meredith's hair. Without those ringlets, it was long and wavy.

Maybe her thought energy had actually worked, Star thought for a moment, but as Meredith took her hand and showed her around the room, telling her the names of each of about fifty baby dolls and stuffed animals and the circumstances of her acquiring each one (the Barbie with the sapphire blue dress was nowhere in sight), Star felt a growing uneasiness.

Meredith's excitement frightened her. Something terrible had happened in that bathroom. Star had known it when she'd found her. Her absence and the teachers' talk had confirmed it. Whatever that boy had done to her, it had to have been bad indeed for her grandma to come get Star though only a few days had passed since she'd said she was done with Star indefinitely.

Those tiny explosions must have just fizzled out in her head like dud supernovas. Concentration alone was not enough.

Meredith said, "I know! Let's swim!"

"I don't have my suit."

"You can borrow one of mine." Meredith pulled her golden yellow dress over her head, and Star stared at Meredith's beige belly and imagined it growing to the size of a watermelon. Meredith stepped into a red suit, which was dotted with flowers. Star changed into a purple ruffled suit that was tight. She left her clothes on Meredith's bedroom floor.

Meredith took Star's hand and led her to the backyard pool.

"You two be careful," Star's grandma said as they passed through the living room. She was on the couch, her arms wrapped tightly around Mrs. Goobis, whose head was slumped onto Star's grandma's shoulder like a brick.

Star suddenly wanted to throw herself into her grandma's lap and beg her forgiveness.

As they stepped out into the sunshine, Star turned to Meredith and said, "Don't worry, Meredith. I'm going to resolve your troubles."

Meredith scrunched her eyes at Star. She ran and jumped into the deep end, creating a large splash, then swam toward the diving board where various noodle floats rested along the ledge like bloated snakes.

Star walked over to the shallow end and submersed herself slowly. Waist deep, she turned her back to Meredith. She opened her backpack where it sat on the ledge, and she pulled out Willie Nelson, concealing him from Meredith's view. She kissed Willie's warm body and looked into his red eye, gritting her teeth so she wouldn't cry. Then she looked up toward the face of the sun, and she whispered, "I'm here, God. Just like Abraham. I'm proving my faith."

She lowered Willie until his body just grazed the water.

"Come on, God," she said as she wept silently. "If you're really out there, then it's your turn. You're supposed to stop me now." But she felt like June Beetle at the zoo. Everywhere she looked, there was nothing but rocks and concrete and empty cages.

Star submerged Willie slowly, millimeter by millimeter. Her arms trembled with the effort to give God every chance she could. When she pressed Willie's face into the water, he clawed and bit her, his long teeth piercing the flesh between her thumb and forefinger. But God, he was silent.

She knew then that she couldn't save Meredith any more than she could help the virgins in heaven. So she did what she could: She saved Willie.

OF ALL THE ANIMALS
IN THE AQUARIUM

Mama loves the sea jellies best.

"See the way the bell goes blub blub?" she says to Robby, pointing to the opaque body of one of the moon jellies. "They pull the water in and push it out, just like pumping blood. Water is their blood. It's how jellies get oxygen and other nutrients."

Mama talks to Robby like he understands.

"Our hearts would make graceful swimmers, too," she says. "Pluck them from our bodies and set them free in the ocean, and they'd move with the water rather than cut through it the way fish do."

A worried pout crumples Robby's face. He claws at the waistband of Mama's skirt, nearly undressing her. When she pries his fingers away, he pinches the soft flesh above her elbow and kisses it. He bends and kisses her knees, then wraps himself around one of her calves. He's seven. Mama says this phase will pass, but she's been saying that since he was born.

If Mama's heart is the bell of a sea jelly, then Robby's is the tentacles.

Mama and Robby aren't a moon jelly with its sleek bell and delicate tentacles like fringe bangs. They're a lion's mane jelly, the largest sea jelly known to humans. The bell can grow seven feet wide, the tentacles 120 feet long. The plaque beside the tank shows a photograph of an adult: It looks like a disembodied breast, trailing wild, stringy milk ducts.

Sometimes Mama tells Robby to give her space, but other times, like now, she rubs the back of his head and smiles bittersweet, like maybe it's not all bad being clung to. Or maybe she's remembering how when Robby was a baby, nothing calmed him as much as her depositing him onto Dad's bare chest, like into a nest. He'd curl his tiny, red fingers around those wooly hairs, and his face would soften into a cool pink.

Eight months ago, not quite ten months after Dad died, in Iraq, Mama started dating. She shoos us out of the house when one of them calls. She says it's so she can hear, but I think it's so she can chalk up Robby's moaning and hollering to the neighbors, street noise.

Years ago, after Aunt Laura's divorce, Mama told her not to worry about dating with two kids: "You have two beautiful little girls. They're assets, not deficits." Greta and Bea were five and four then and had shiny black hair and olive skin and singing voices so sweet, strangers cried during their duets at school recitals.

I never was pretty like my cousins. Puberty hasn't helped. Mama jokes that my skin and hair are so oily, I better steer clear of flames or I'll ignite. Then she says not to worry, she went through the same thing. It's a phase. It'll pass.

But some mornings, she winces at me like she does at the bathroom mirror when she's tweezing gray hairs. She says, "Thirteen, thirteen. How can I be old enough to be the mother of a thirteen-year-old?"

Before Dad died, I was just Ann—not a teenager, not a deficit. I guess you could say Robby has always been a deficit, but Mama wouldn't say that aloud, not even now.

I know Mama has lost another man, because we don't come to the aquarium on good days: when she stays out until one in the morning, then wakes up early to make chocolate chip pancakes. A few days ago, she bought a brand new dress, red, for dancing in, she said. But the dress's only action last night was the breeze from the ceiling fan while we ate Frito pie and watched an old Julia Roberts movie, Mama bouncing Robby on her lap to keep him quiet.

Mama says she doesn't want to date, that dating is, in fact, the last thing she wants to do, but if she doesn't look for a man now, when? She's not getting any younger, she says.

She makes dating sound like buying a new blender, which she did a few months ago. The broken blender had been a wedding gift. She had it fourteen years. "I'd give anything to have it restored, but nobody seems to know how to fix anything anymore. Me included. And what am I going to do? I have to have a blender," she said. The blenders in the store all had plastic pitchers, even the expensive ones. "I don't want plastic. It stains. It smells," Mama said, but after visiting three different stores, and finding only one brand that made glass pitchers and their price tags being nearly three times that of the plastic pitcher models, she gave in and bought plastic.

Mama doesn't say, if only …. But it's us she's thinking of when she says that her heart would swim as gracefully as a sea jelly if it were set free.

I know because now Robby is howling and punching the moon jelly tank, and Mama has to remove him from the glass like he's suctioned to it. She has to take him outside to the bench across from the huge wooden shark's mouth. Kids enter through a black curtain around back to pose for photos, their faces lodged between the shark's teeth like bits of food debris. Mama rocks Robby while other mothers watch out of the corners of their eyes, while they whisper to their kids in harsh voices not to poke the glass.

I know because while Mama rocks Robby, I remain where I am, in front of the Bay pipefish tank. The plaque says the slender pipefish have to anchor themselves to the eelgrasses because they're poor swimmers. They'd perish in the open coastal waters. Still, I admire how they blend in effortlessly. You have to lean in close to pick them out. It's the eyes like tiny gold washers set in tar that give them away.

CINÉMA VÉRITÉ

"Just a little chemo," my mother said. She'd called from the interstate as she crossed the Arizona state line from New Mexico. She was going to be in the hospital for a while and wanted me to keep Jaspers. In the most recent photograph I'd seen of her, my mother sat on a boulder, her knees pressed together in the manner of a child posing for a school portrait; the dog sat perched on her lap. My mother had sunglasses pushed back into her thinning tobacco-colored hair, the dog a bandana around its neck. They both wore sugar-skull grins that made you inadvertently check your own face in the mirror to make sure it didn't reveal some defect of character you strained to suppress.

She didn't cross just one state line to put me in this fix—she crossed four. She would've crossed five if she'd taken the shorter route through the Texas Panhandle, but she said, "You'd have to sever my legs and arms before you'd manage to drag me into *that* state." And no doubt she still wouldn't have gone without a fight. She would've wielded a knife between her teeth like Prince Randian in Tod Browning's *Freaks*.

"Sorry to hear that, Mom, I really am, but I can't keep your dog," I said.

I hadn't seen my mother in over a dozen years, not since I was a senior in college. I flew out to spend spring break with her where she'd been working in Portland. The trip had been a whimsy, a gamble. I had no reason to expect it to go well, but foolishly, fantastically, I'd imagined something cinematic: a pan of us trolling downtown streets arm in arm, a medium shot of us people-watching at a café, a close-up of lattés blooming foam. Too many film studies courses will do that to you. I longed for cinematic details though that sort of life couldn't possibly spawn from my family's gene pool. Or really I just longed for what my friends seemed to take for granted—a mother who called from time to time to inquire about courses and dating prospects and the food in my dorm refrigerator, who was something more than a name I had to produce to apply for a credit card.

In reality, the only coffee my mother drank was instant from a rectangular canister. She worked every day of my visit, each morning offering me cereal paired with a ten-dollar bill. She had me drop her off at the nursing home so that I could sightsee during the days. On my third brunch visit that week to the vegan restaurant down the street from her apartment, one of the waiters asked me out. Such was my self-loathing that I accompanied him to a strip club (my idea), then gave him a blow job (his idea) in the back seat of my mother's car.

Crushed, I returned to school and moped about the snow-lined campus. Graduation weekend, I told everyone my mother had won a trip to Antarctica in a sweepstakes. Then I made a decision. No more expectations concerning my mother. No more delusions. I wouldn't cut her off entirely, but I wouldn't offer anything or expect anything.

"The cat will have a conniption fit," I said now.

"So put Jaspers outside. He'll be OK outside."

I reminded her that this was the desert, that he'd be lucky to last a day outside what with the heat and the scorpions and rattlesnakes.

"You don't know Jaspers. He's tough like me. He'll survive." This wasn't cancer patient rhetoric. My mother had long postured as some kind of vigilante hero rescuing herself from the daily onslaught of shit slung in her direction. When she started working as a nurse a few years after my sister Natalie started kindergarten, every evening from then on was graced by war stories about people—patients, nurses, doctors, the kitchen lady—who tried unsuccessfully to cut my mother down. She reminded us that she tolerated none of it. "I stick up for myself," she said. And her eyes were so wide and her gestures so spastic during the retelling that I half expected her head to spin all the way around or a spring to pop out from somewhere—that her body might self-destruct like a robot on the fritz.

"What about Natalie?" I asked now.

Natalie was the ongoing recipient of my mother's care packages and checks though she was past thirty. When cornered, Natalie pontificated about her volunteer work to save the sea turtles, but it was clear to everyone, perhaps even our mother, that most of her time was devoted to marathon bacchanalian beach parties.

Fort Lauderdale was probably half the distance from Tennessee.

She said, "I don't want her to know about this. Your sister's sensitive." She was silent for a moment. "He's got nowhere else to go, Fran. If you won't take him for me, I'm going to have to leave him at a shelter. They'd put him to sleep. I love that dog to death. It would kill me."

The last time my mother reentered my life, it was via a box with three wrapped gifts, their respective tags reading "Happy Birthday 2003," "Merry Christmas 2003," and "Happy Birthday 2004." Soon after, she called to ask if I'd steal some photo albums and a gadget called the Spa Master from my father's house. The time before that was when Greg and I got married. She sent a voucher for one night in a hotel in St. Louis (a sweepstakes winning, no doubt), a silver heart-shaped plaque reading "George and Fran, October 2000" (which Greg hung above our toilet in an effort to cheer me up), and a brief note explaining that she'd rather be a knife-thrower's apprentice than be in the same room as my father and his sisters, but that she loved me more than I would ever know and would I pester my father about a piece of furniture that was rightfully hers?

This time the request for a favor came without gifts, it seemed.

It was August, and the desert summer heat pummeled every living thing into drunken submission, so perhaps that's why I eventually agreed to meet my mother in a Denny's parking lot (she didn't ask to come to the house, and I didn't offer). Also, I was intrigued by her proclaimed devotion to this dog. I wanted to call her bluff. I was certain she wouldn't be back for him, and I thought that proving myself right could be satisfying in some way.

When I arrived, my business-as-usual mother popped the trunk and unloaded a lot more than Jaspers onto me. There were gifts after all. She'd brought along aerobics videos, eight boxes of Girl Scout cookies (half of them opened), a bona fide longhorn skull, cake decorating supplies, an unopened disco globe, and a suitcase full of Jaspers' possessions: leopard-print bed, canned food, kibble, treats, ear medicine, toothbrush and toothpaste, claw clippers, and a dozen or so candy-colored rubber mammals, all with great big smiling mouths. They looked like novelty sex toys.

"Just some stuff I was getting rid of and thought you might like," she explained as she piled it all onto the asphalt between our cars. If I didn't take her junk, it would sit there until someone else did or else a Denny's employee was tasked with the job of disposing of it.

What I said was, "I'm not brushing that dog's teeth."

"That's OK. I've only done it a couple times myself. I brought everything he owns, just in case."

"Just in case what?" She had dark circles under her eyes, but that wasn't new, nor was the way she mostly avoided eye contact and took every opportunity to crack her neck. What was new, at least since I'd last seen her, was the extra padding around her middle—fifteen pounds' worth probably.

Without blinking, she said, "I thought maybe you brushed that cat's teeth, that maybe you might know how to do it. I really should brush his teeth. He just hates it so much, and I don't know what I'm doing."

"If you don't come back for him, I'm not keeping him," I said.

She shook her head. Then she reached in and lifted the dog from where he lay on the driver's seat, no doubt still warm from my mother's body. She pressed him to her chest, scratched his neck, and rubbed noses with him. He whimpered, and she cooed. When she did look at me, she looked pained. She said, "I don't know why you'd say something like that."

"Now you take care of yourself, boy," she said to the dog. "Mama loves you."

"I'll be in touch," she said to me as she placed the dog into my arms as gently and carefully as if handing me an organ from her own body.

On the drive home, I turned the volume on the radio up higher than I had in years. To muffle the dog's cries, I told myself.

A few weeks later a man named Clayton Stanley called at half-past four in the morning on a Saturday to inform me he'd broken up with my mother.

The night before, I'd watched Don Siegel's *Invasion of the Body Snatchers*, so I watched Greg carefully that morning as he put on his running shoes and then circled the bedroom five times searching for his eyeglasses. If he'd found them any sooner, I might have been suspicious. This was typical Greg, though, even his getting up ridiculously early in the summer to run before there was the desert sun to reckon with. He kissed me and then he was gone, closing the door as gently as he would have if I'd still been asleep. When he first told me he loved me so many years earlier, I'd told him he was joking, this after we'd been sleeping together for three months. The stricken look on his face when I said it was what made me believe him.

Clayton Stanley said he would have broken up with my mother even if she hadn't gotten cancer.

"Good to know," I said.

"Your mother's funny and charming, but she's not easy to be with. She's like a big ball of tangled strands of Christmas lights. Strands that don't go together. You know, like different colors and different shapes. And ornaments and hooks. A heck of a lot of hooks actually. It's more than I'm prepared to handle right now."

"That metaphor is very helpful. Thank you."

Clayton said, "Well, would *you* want to be in a relationship with a person like that?"

Jaspers barked from the guest bedroom. I didn't care what my mother said about it; that pitiful little thing would have been a rattlesnake meal in no time, assuming the heat didn't get him first. Clive, our cat, rose from his place by my feet and buried his face into my neck like a lover.

"I get it," I said. "I suppose that if I could just as easily break up with my mother, I'd do it, too."

"I thought you should check on her. This breakup could be hard for her. Her time is limited, you know."

I didn't know the least little thing about it, I told him. I asked how he got my number.

He told me I was her emergency contact. In her personnel file. They'd worked together. She quit.

Perhaps I shouldn't have been surprised to learn my mother had listed me as her emergency contact. She did drive across five states to leave her dog with me. But I was bewildered, my mind blown. Why should I come to my mother's rescue in the case of an emergency?

But after hanging up the phone, I felt something else— how alone my mother must have been in the world if I was the best she could do for an emergency contact and for saving her beloved dog from euthanasia. Lying there clammy with exhaustion, I felt as though my gut was a sack full of stones and my bones made of air.

First thing Natalie said was, "Cancer! But she's going to be all right, right?"

"Do you think everyone who gets cancer ends up all right?" I said.

"God, you always know what to say," I heard between earfuls of wind.

"That's right," I said. "That's why I called. Since you're the sensitive one, I figured you'd want to travel to Tennessee to look in on her."

She couldn't, she said, and slewed off a list of reasons, finishing with "And I'd be a big sobbing mess. I'd just upset her."

Laughter like the howls of coyotes echoed in the background. A petulant male voice shouted, "Hurry up, Nat!"

Then, "You're the oldest," she said matter-of-factly.

I didn't ask for clarification, but I got it anyway. "The oldest takes care of the parents when they get old." Not a hint of maliciousness in her voice. She could have been explaining something mundane like it was the job of a stem to hold a plant upright.

"Mom's not old," was all I said.

After hanging up the phone, I abandoned the pasta salad I'd been making for dinner and left Greg, who was out rock climbing, a note that I was going to the cinema. I didn't bother to look up what was playing or when, just drove over and bought a ticket to the next film showing. The month's Second Saturdays Horror Classics feature was George Romero's *Night of the Living Dead*.

I was forty minutes early, but the theater was empty, so I sat in the gloaming and waited as strangers slowly trickled in. I could hear people's individual breaths, the intimate sounds of their lips pressing against plastic cups and their fingers searching pockets and purses. Sitting in the dark with a handful of strangers, I half expected someone to lay a hand on my leg or bite my ear. It felt like a one-night stand, like anything could happen.

Then the movie started, and I sucked the chocolate off Junior Mints as I watched the small band of survivors in the boarded-up farmhouse perish one by one. Tom and Judy, the teenage couple, got themselves blown up when Tom spilled gasoline near the truck that Judy was pinned inside of, her jacket caught. Harry and Helen Cooper were devoured by their daughter, Karen, whom they'd foolishly brought into the farmhouse despite the fact that she'd been bit. Barbra was devoured by her brother. And Ben, the only one of the group to survive the night, was shot in the morning by a very human redneck who barely glimpsed him before mistaking him for a monster.

I took the most decadent shower of my life, stood beneath the spray of hot water for fifteen minutes maybe before Greg's knock on the glass door startled me. He was naked and grinning.

I gave him a discouraging look.

He stepped into the shower and wrapped his arms around me. He said, "It's incredibly kind of you to drive all the way out there to check on her. You don't have to do it."

"There isn't anybody else."

"Like I said, incredibly kind."

"I don't feel kind. I feel the opposite of kind."

He lifted my chin up. "You're nothing like her."

"I dreamt last night that she'd committed suicide."

Greg kissed me. "Babe, I'm sorry."

"I haven't told you the half of it. I was relieved, I mean seriously, deeply relieved. I saw myself at her funeral in a black skirt that ended in stiff ruffles and when Natalie said to me that I was unfeeling, I said to her, 'Death is just a part of life.' And then I ate a shrimp cocktail."

"You can't be held responsible for your dreams. Everybody dreams crazy shit."

I didn't tell him then how much like a Jean-Luc Godard film my dream had been. Stark black-and-white with jump cuts, collages, and asynchronicity. I could sketch that ruffled skirt in detail, as well as the shot of the three shrimp hooked over the rim of a martini glass framed by an arched doorway looking onto my mother's coffin. I didn't tell him how exquisitely beautiful the dream had been. I didn't tell him how disappointed I'd felt when I woke and it was all over.

My mother's apartment building had bars on the windows, and the peeling forest green doors were swollen from humidity. The porches looked out on the parking lot that surrounded the building on all sides. And on my mother's side of the building, there was the additional fascination of a feed store across the street with all its pick-up trucks and stiff bricks of hay. On her porch was where I found my mother—kicking back on a fold-out chair, a glass of iced tea sweating in her hand.

Jaspers was out of the car, between the thin metal bars of the porch railing, and onto my mother's lap before I could shut the car door. My mother smiled in spite of herself. She held the dog up to get a good look at him.

"You didn't tell me you were coming," she said. "I can't take Jaspers back right now. It's not possible."

"It's just a visit," I said.

"You drove twenty-plus hours so he could visit?"

"There is the whole chemo/cancer thing. And you don't answer your phone. And your coworker called me."

She looked at me briefly, then back at the dog.

"Well, I've changed my mind." She cracked her neck.

"About what?"

"About chemo. Pathetic odds. I'm more likely to win a million dollars from a nickel slot machine."

"So what are you going to do?" I asked.

"Dig for diamonds."

At first I thought it was a joke. Talk about dismal odds. But then she disappeared into the apartment and returned with a pamphlet for Arkansas's Crater of Diamonds State Park, which boasts a 37-acre mine field where about 700 diminutive diamonds are discovered each year.

"Until you die?" I said. If I'd thought about it more, I might have worded it differently. Might have.

"Yes, I'm going to dig myself a grave." She grinned.

This was a woman who'd spent her weekends when I was a girl trolling the beach looking like an extra from the cantina scene in *Star Wars* with her metal detector extending from one arm like a strange proboscis, a shovel in her other hand, and earphones that made her ears over into the compound eyes of a fly. In the evenings, she'd addressed post card after post card to enter every sweepstakes imaginable.

That's probably when I should have asked her how long she'd been told to expect or, heck, where in her body the cancer was. I couldn't tell from looking at her. Other than the extra weight, no visible part of her was misshapen. Nothing fluttered or murmured. She didn't hold herself any differently or rub away at a fixed region the way pregnant women do the foreign growths inside their bodies. But I didn't ask. I didn't want to know. Asking questions can get a person into trouble. You often get a good deal more than you bargain for, and I was on the hook enough as it was.

What I asked was when she planned to leave.

"You might as well give me a ride now since you're here," she said. "It's on your way back."

After she'd quit her job, she'd sold her car. She'd been planning this for a while, no doubt—bit by bit, getting rid of everything that wasn't practical to take with her to Murfreesboro, including Clayton Stanley. She'd probably never planned on chemo in the first place. It was a ruse to get me to take Jaspers in—more effective than saying, I'm going to run off to a pit in Arkansas to treasure hunt until I die. It turned out I was sort of right about her abandoning the dog, but I was wrong about it giving me some satisfaction. She hadn't planned on telling me any of this. She would have disappeared into thin air if Clayton hadn't called and I hadn't driven out there pronto.

All that was left to do was pack her clothing. So that's what I did while she walked Jaspers. None of it was folded in its current state—wadded in drawers, flung over the door frame of the closet. The abundant wrinkles made folding seem pointless. Still, I folded each piece as if each fold were a punch on my responsibilities-toward-my-dying-mother punch card, which, once filled, would earn me absolution from the nuisances of guilt and regret. I folded five pairs of elastic-waistband polyester slacks, more or less identical except for the colors; six blouses, a hodgepodge of pastels and neutrals, similarly plain and awkward like an aspiring sewer's first projects; four faded T-shirts; two cotton nightgowns and a robe, all ankle-length; a single beige bra;

an assortment of ankle socks; and a stack of beige cotton briefs. They weren't clothes that would catch someone's eye on a rack. They didn't look exactly comfortable, either. They were cheap, there was that, but if frugality was all there was to it, she could have done better at a thrift store. What they revealed was someone who didn't think about clothing except to register that it was necessary to wear some if you didn't want to get arrested.

I loaded the canvas suitcase, as well as a pile of bedding and several cardboard boxes I found in the kitchen—toiletries, snack foods (mostly cheese crackers and caramel popcorn), and digging supplies—into the trunk of my car. As I closed the trunk, a voice called out from a neighboring porch sliding glass door. "LuAnn, you taking off already?"

My mother had come around the corner of the building, the dog strolling beside her on his leash. "My daughter showed up. She's going to give me a ride."

"I know you weren't going to leave without saying good-bye," the voice hollered, and out into the sunlight pouring onto the porch stepped a transsexual in a tangerine silk robe. She was tall and angular, and she touched her smooth scalp as though she hadn't intended for anyone to see it in its naked state. She'd sacrificed vanity to say farewell to my mother, who laughed in response.

"Oh, you're so funny," my mother said. I didn't see what was so funny, but the woman returned my mother's laugh and threw her arms up in the air.

"Woman, get over here and give me a proper hug good-bye."

My mother laughed again, but when the woman grasped her firmly by the shoulder blades, she quieted and hugged her back. I mean my mother gripped her like a lost child returned.

My mother was *not* a hugger; she was a patter. And I remembered her complaining to us when I was a kid about a transsexual at the nursing home she'd worked at, how she'd used the women's restroom. *I have no problem with any of it but the bathroom part. I just can't relax if I know there's a penis in the next stall.*

Suddenly I wanted to back out. I wanted to get into my car and drive all the way home, leaving my mother to take the bus. I didn't want to be alone with her. Breathing in lungfuls of particles that had traveled in and out of the mucus-lined passages of my mother's body seemed far too intimate.

Driving the four hours to Murfreesboro with my mother as passenger was like tending to a pigeon that had flown in through the window. She squawked and squirmed for several minutes as she situated herself. Once settled, she gnashed caramel popcorn and rubbed the dog so fiercely I worried he might bite her. She stared straight ahead at the road. She remained in the car when I stopped for gas, declined my suggestion that she stretch her legs or take advantage of the restroom.

Arriving in Murfreesboro was a relief, and then it wasn't. The cabin my mother planned to spend her remaining days in was rustic to say the least. The only running water was a spigot outside the building. Toilets and showers were communal and located down the street. The beds were wooden platforms on which you could set up a sleeping bag or some blankets. It was equipped with a single outlet, but no light, no fan. Forget about a refrigerator.

She unpacked her suitcase and her boxes onto one of the four wooden platforms, arranged everything in neat little rows that I would bet didn't last more than twenty-four hours. She talked aloud to herself about where each item should go.

I excused myself to go to the restroom down the street. There I splashed cold water onto my face. In the worn mirror I could see how much I looked like her. Same creases under the eyes, same crooked mouth. If I'd felt like smiling, I would have seen her smiling back at me. Although normally I thought cosmetic surgery was for cyborgs and people utterly lacking in self-worth, at that moment, I kind of got it. Why should anyone be doomed every day to stare back at the features of the people who conceived them?

When I returned to the cabin, I said, "Mom, this place." What? It stinks? You shouldn't die here? And if not, where? My house?

"I don't need much."

"What about food? What if it gets very hot? Summer isn't over yet. What if you get very sick?"

"I'm already sick."

"You know what I mean."

"I won't suffer," she said. She sounded fierce and practiced as though she'd repeated these words to herself. "That's why I'm here. No hospitals. No treatments. I'll be out before I can count to ten. As for food, there's a cafeteria at the Visitor's Center. And you can take me to the store to buy a fan if it makes you feel better."

If it makes me feel better? Was this judgment? Or was she simply assuaging me? I decided I didn't care either way. A fan *would* make me feel better.

Despite her protests, I insisted on purchasing the fan, as well as every kind of snack imaginable and cases of water and a whole lot else. I went on a shopping spree. I bought her a lamp, a solar-powered lantern for trips to the bathroom in the dark, a battery-powered radio and three packages of batteries. I pestered her to pick out some books and magazines. And did she want a portable DVD player and movies? And heck, how about some art supplies? Might she want to take up watercolor or pastels? And gum? Did she need chewing gum?

Now my mother was the one who was worried.

"This isn't like you," she said.

I surprised myself by throwing my arms around her right then and there in the checkout line. My mother felt like limp celery in my arms, but I squeezed her anyway. I squeezed her until she said she couldn't breathe. When I let go, she dug around in her purse, muttering about something she couldn't find. I looked away, too, so that she wouldn't see the pain in my eyes.

I knew then that I had no intention of staying the night. I was spending money like the apocalypse was upon us because it kind of was. I was going to leave my mother to die alone in a rustic-as-rustic-gets cabin in Arkansas. I was trying to buy some kind of absolution though I knew that not even buying her the moon would be enough.

But I was *not* Karen Cooper rising from the dead and doing her mother Helen off with a masonry trowel, then feasting upon her flesh. I was Helen Cooper revised. I was walking out and driving away. I was saving myself.

When we returned to the cabin, we had two hours before the park closed, so after unloading the car for the second time that day and giving Jaspers some treats and a brief jaunt outside the cabin, we headed to the park with my mother's diamond digging supplies in tow.

As the sun grew heavier, my mother poured dirt onto her sifting screen, shook it back and forth, fingered the pieces remaining, dumped, and repeated. I knelt down with her despite how uncomfortable the grit would be on my legs and arms and in my shoes as I drove later that evening—getting as far away from her as possible before stopping to rest for the night.

Then I watched her make her way over to the washing station, a long shot that included a panoramic view of the grapefruit-pink sunset and the people scattered about digging and sifting through thirty-seven acres of dirt for the two minuscule diamonds odds predicted would be discovered that day. Then a medium-shot of her standing among a small crowd of earnest diamond hunters washing and agitating their screens together. Then an iris-in that narrowed further and further until all I could see was my mother's head tilted back in a wild laugh, an image that would break anybody's heart.

TRANSACTIONS

My mother stands outside the extended-stay hotel with her enormous dog as I pull into the parking lot. She's short on rent. Eight hundred dollars this time.

A few dozen words in almost as many years, and she left a voicemail message saying she was worried about *me*. "I can't get a hold of you. Everything OK?"

She requested I leave the cash loan in an envelope at the hotel's reception. Just write her name on it. The money would be safe, she said. All this to avoid looking me in the eye.

I wouldn't let her off so easily.

Walking the dog is her next best defense. She hopes I'll produce the money though my rolled-down window. She'll repeat that somebody else is to blame. I'll say, don't worry about it. I'll drive away.

But I ask to use her bathroom.

Following her up the stairs, I see how much her hair has thinned. The dog lumbers up the steps between us, its size impossible, like Paul Bunyan's ox.

Her apartment smells like dog and urine, hopefully also dog.

"I'm going to try to sell that table," my mother says. "It's real heavy. It's good quality."

The table in question is stone—meant for a patio, not indoor dining. Catalogues, advertisements, and credit card applications blanket its surface. On top, a jug of fruit punch and a bag of sweetened corn puffs, junk food marketed to children.

"Unless *you* want it," she says.

I don't want any of this. What I want is as realistic as a pumpkin carriage.

She points me to the bathroom.

Atop a tower of plastic drawers stuffed with cosmetics sit two bald Styrofoam heads and a pile of wigs, each one inside out. The mirror is cloudy and scratched as though something clawed its way inside its own reflection. Or maybe the reflection clawed its way out.

"Keep being bad, Buddy, and you'll earn your way back into the cage," my mother says in the other room.

A voice on the radio exalts heartbreak.

I write down everything. Details are my inheritance.

CPSIA information can be obtained
at www.ICGtesting.com
Printed in the USA
FFHW02n2239141018
48773655-52887FF

9 780913 785881